Best Wishes

Tolomay's World and The Pool of Light

M.E. Lorde

TOLOMAY'S WORLD
And
The Pool of Light
(Book One in the **Tolomay's World** series)

M.E. Lorde

Tolomay's World and The Pool of Light

M.E. Lorde

PRAISE FOR M.E. LORDE'S
TOLOMAY'S WORLD
and
The Pool of Light
(Book One of the Tolomay's World
Series)

'I could not put this book down.'
-B.M.L.

'Great balance of warmth in characters.
Adventure- good VS evil-greed. I've found it
so hard over the last several years to find
books that capture and keep my interest- so
this series is wonderful. I'm anxious to read
what happens next.'
N.Venn

'So unique, this book should be a movie. I
could not sleep until I finished it.'
V. Smith

I couldn't put this book down! There's plenty
of action. Plenty of romance. And plenty of
surprises!!!
Grace B.D.

A Paper Airplanes Publishing Book/Published by
arrangement with the author.

Tolomay's World
and the Pool of Light

By M.E. Lorde

Library of Congress Catalog Card Number 2012900610
ISBN-13: 978-0983715955
ISBN-10: 0983715955

Manufactured in the United States of America
This book is a work of fiction. Names, characters, places or
incidents are either products of the author's imagination or, if
real are used fictitiously. Any resemblance to actual events,
locales, or persons, living or dead, is coincidental.

M.E. Lorde

For my sunshine girl,

Kayla
~You are my inspiration~

TOLOMAY'S WORLD

and

The Pool of Light

(Book One)

Tolomay's World is written in a language called *Merican.* Don't let it throw you. This diatribe varies little from American English, in that it contains slightly altered syntax.

This novel is also written from two point of views. ChapTers with a capitalized T in the heading are from Tolomay's perspective. When the word *Chapter* appears without a capital T, then the point of view is omniscient: the all-knowing eye.

Tolomay's World and The Pool of Light

~Character Definitions~

Tolomay Ramey- First person to swim through the Pool of Light. Referred to as one of the 'Originals'. Curation and Herbal expert.

Tarron Quoia Ramey- Tolomay's father. Creator of Vision Fold and the Pool of Light.

Carmella- Tolomay's pet lizard and constant companion.

Bear- Large brown bear- pesky, terrifying, and life-threatening.

Kenter- First male entering the clean world. Expert in solar energy, metallurgy, electronics, electricity and mechanics. Twin to Lethia.

Lethia- Carpentry architecture expert. Twin to Kenter.

Arden- Rule breaker. Kenter's best friend.

Sandra Lockley- Beautiful girl who shamelessly chases (stalks) Kenter.

Senator Lockley- Sandra's father. Doesn't like Kenter.

Professor Mize Maxy- Head of Science Division. Selected Kenter for the swim.

Professor Michael Manngie- Lethia's geometry teacher.

M.E. Lorde

M.E. Lorde

ChapTer One

"Peace of life," said the chideman as he poured the blue water from the glass urn into the pool. It was surreal.

"Peace of life." My response was automatic.

My heart pounded. For thirteen years I'd trained for this. Still I was not ready. The machine's copper pipes gave off a warm smell that drifted to my nostrils as if precious biscuits were baking in the eating room. The calming scent only made it worse. I was leaving.

On display before every citizen in the community, my bare feet stepped the few inches further to the edge of the pool. Fear haunted my mind. Shivering from head to toe caused my short golden dress to tickle at the tops of my thighs. I brushed away the itch. Goose bumps peppered my arms and legs. I was freezing. For a moment, the massive musics and sounds on the stage overwhelmed me. I was small in comparison to everything here, all present and to this wondrous event. Through dazed thoughts, my focus returned and I remembered to count to three before placing my foot in the shallow liquid.

With eyes watering, my every heartbeat echoed in my ears. Never again would my father's eyes look upon me. Never again would I feel his warm embrace. I would so miss his gentle, loving voice. How would I bear it? I fought my great desire to turn and dart to him, or steal a look as he sat in his chair upon the stage. Instead, I kept my step.

There would not be another last goodbye. We already said it, and he wanted just the one. It would be my greatest honor to him to leave with the dignity, respect, and position he bestowed upon me, to act older than my meager thirteen years. I had to be brave and pave the way for the others, as he had instructed.

The tears nearly choked me as I

quietly sniffed them back. I could scarcely see, but chose not to rub the wet away. Everyone would notice. More would only follow and my eyes would be closed soon enough. The time had arrived. This was no longer wholly my choice. I was being led by my duty and so had to control my emotions for these last few seconds.

The immaculate stage held static, causing the miniscule hairs on my head to stand on end. They reached toward the beautiful colored glass of the cathedral roof in the pod community's grandest room, as if they too wanted to stay. The urge to run, to escape, consumed me, yet I betrayed my heart, followed my learned directions, and kept my course.

No matter the logic and knowledge in my head, nothing had prepared me for this feeling of claws tearing me apart from the inside out. I fought off the nausea. I could not be ill, not in front of the community while representing my father.

The crystal and copper Pool of Light lay before the five of us, with solar panels running from floor to ceiling as the toner's chorus continued to sing behind us. The brilliant round majesty beneath my feet, only six inches deep, held the key to our futures and to what would become the whole of humanity. We were taking these steps for everyone. Once we left, we could never return home.

Tarron had ordered that we space ourselves just two paces separated, one behind the next. The four older candidates followed behind me, the taste of anticipation mingling with the hum of energy that filled the great room. My mind whirled.

'Keep walking forward... do not turn around,' father's words echoed in my head.

I was horrified. Chills took residence up and down my spine, causing me to shake further. How would my days unfold without him by my side? How could I leave him alone? My heart was dying.

'The coming light can blind, if you lose protection of your eyelids,' he had warned.

Think only of your training and the swim, I reprimanded myself against my inert weakness. *Focus. You are leading the others.*

I squeezed my eyes closed.

"Your eyes… don't forget," I choked out the words, reminding the four following me to keep theirs closed as well.

The desire to see where my feet landed was nearly more than I could endure as I took my next step. Blindly, trembling as I'd never thought possible, I walked on until a humming of energy engulfed me. Then a wall of water, warm and flowing, caressed my face and arms and legs until I was drenched in it. It unnerved me. I imagined my skin would feel this way if covered with a million tiny insects. That vision sent more shivers. I rubbed away the feeling. Fear controlled me. I was holding my breath. *'Do not forget to breathe, Tolomay,'* I remembered father's training. *'Or you may lose consciousness.'*

Barely able to manage my thoughts, I took back my air and continued forward.

A light penetrated the liquid as if they were one and the same. Much too bright, even with eyes closed, it rained down upon my body as if it were the sun and had no limits. The burning lasted only a moment and rid me of my chills. Then I was struck hard in the back by a force that seemed more as power than matter. It propelled me through the air so fast I almost opened my eyes, but instead fell into a somersault, ending in a stand as I had been trained.

The grasses felt soft beneath my bare feet. The air smelled completely different... fresh and clean. Was it safe to look? Sure the diminished music meant safety, I slowly peeked to see what tickled my toes. My feet rested on an unbelievable world of vegetation. I turned my eyes upward. Plant life flourished about me. An insect landed on a bloom and dipped its head inside until completely hidden in the bright yellow flower.

With every cell overwhelmed, my delight leapt. Miraculous science! Holy green gravity, it was unbelievable. We did it! I accomplished what I trained my entire life to do!

Magnificent and abundant life surrounded me as far as I could see. The sky was a magical light blue like the ancient's paintings and pictures; the clouds were bright whites and grays. It had all been true, or was I dreaming?

As hard as it was for my mind to accept my surroundings, I could no longer hold my tears. Crying like a joyous newborn, I breathed in the pure nature of the heaven of the clean world. Its power bore into my soul. The energy of a long sturdy tree line reached toward me in the wind, welcoming my spirit to share in this wondrous space. I looked to the trees' highest branches. They were much taller than I had imagined.

This was real. Father's machine worked! We were here!

The much too-loud screech of the hole and noise of the water pouring into this world drowned out the distant sound of the toner's chorus. My heart shook with uncontrolled excitement.

"We made it!" I shouted over the machines deafening pitch, then turned to view the light point from which I had come.

But... where were the others?

The water fell from midair, waiting for them. As if in warning the sound turned to something altogether different. First came the silence, and then an angry hiss. Elation left me as the air around the running water shifted to a dingy gray.

Impending doom gripped my chest as Candra's face peered through the wall of water. She smiled in disbelief at the world she saw. Why had the pool not spit her out? Why did it hold her to itself? Dread filled my belly even before I heard her shrill scream.

With half her body through, she hovered just ten feet away, her arms stretched toward me. The look of astonishment fled from her face as she let out a sound more horrific than I'd ever heard. Terrified, my mind blanked, body froze. We had no training of this otherworldly power. A moment later, Teresa was at her side, next Florentina, and finally Marva. They did not clear the entryway either and instead, floated helplessly as the glorious and glowing blue water turned a dirty brown.

The scent of a burned out candle permeated the air. Candra's skin was pulling light from the water into itself. Every blood vessel seeped its treasure from her skin. The others bled, too. Nearly instantly, they were painted in crimson. No longer lit, the water turned as dark as an endless hole and the black backdrop taunted us all. Panicked, I barked the order.

"HURRY! MOVE! MOVE!" I screamed, but none of us obeyed.

Unable to aide them the slightest bit, I stood shocked at their suffering when a brilliant flash of light struck the portal. Their shrieks filled me with horror as I watched them writhe frantically in the midair, black watery grave. Like the dark liquid that hung motionless, the moment was frozen in time. Candra stopped screaming. She was gone.

No! No! No!

Mere seconds dragged like eternity as Teresa's voice took on a high pitched squeal. Her eyes nearly bulged from her head. I viewed my team members disappear, sucked into nothingness as the Pool of Light made a sizzling sound. Then it slammed shut with a thunderous *clap.* The water disappeared and I stared at the now empty space in the beautiful green world, my face awash in tears.

What just happened? Nothing could be real. I lost them all, lost all who I'd known, those in my charge. Finally, my feet led me running toward the closed light point. I grasped frantically at the air before me.

"Come back! Come back!" The words choked. "Father, take me back! I want to come home!" I sobbed. "Bring me home! I'm sorry! I'm sorry!"

I gave way to gravity and fell as a lost spirit to the trembling Earth.

With my cheek against the cool earth, tears dried in the warm breeze. The feeling haunted me. Why had I not reached out to my team when they were in unfathomable pain? I was the curer, the healer, yet stood idly by and watched them each die. I'd failed my life's purpose, to lead and keep safe and healthy all citizens in the new community. Guilt annihilated my soul.

"I'm so sorry," I bawled as if they could hear a single word of it.

Crumpled into a ball, I wailed to the enormous trees, now wholly and utterly alone in this strange green world. Why had I lived?

ChapTer Two

What did it mean to be in love with the world? I could not tell a soul. For it had been long for me, too long. Not that the passion was dead in me. It was alive and well and screamed at me each day from the first sign of sunlight, until I closed my eyes to sleep. This place was more than I'd thought, but the isolation made it impossible to share things with anyone else. It was my birthday and, once again, I spent it alone.

Three years is too long to be alone on this Earth, even with Carmella at my side.

I first saw her after the blast, the one that took the others. Even while the ground shook, Carmella sat looking at me as she did now. It was as if she instinctively knew what it did to them, as if she knew there would be no others but me from then on out.

Without a blink or so much as a shiver, she sat frozen on that rock, looking at me with those heavy lidded eyes. That day I cried for hours, longer than I cared to recall. Carmella did not know of self pity. Pity does not help a creature who's struggling alone to survive in the wild.

She was a different breed, but we were friends, two females living together as silent partners, Carmella and I, lizard and gardener. We relied on each other. I liked to think it she had the nature of truly caring for me, aside from the insects I fed her. Garden crickets were her favorite and in ample supply on the hillside.

Not those little green ones, mind you, but the big black ones that squirmed in her mouth and crackled as she swallowed them whole. They were too big for her, but none the less, she gobbled them up even while they caused her to choke.

The lizard would never learn not to bite off more than she could chew, but who would blame her? Perhaps crickets were her chocolate. It'd been so long since my taste of chocolate. Something as diminutive as a little choking would not have prevented me from inhaling a chunk of the sweet brown heaven, if one were available in this place. I'd have devoured it.

So there I was waiting with Carmella, each Tuesday the same routine. Even in oblivion, consistency ruled the planet. Tarron told us it would be like this. He said the waiting would be grueling, though he himself had never and could never swim in the light; he was too old. But he was right. The waiting *was* hard and you could not train for that.

I prepared myself for three months before my swim, isolated myself whenever possible from the rest of the group. I stayed in my room, ate alone, camped for three weeks straight in the wooded side of the lab's property. I did it right, just as Tarron trained me to. I thought I was ready when the time came to take the step. I thought I was. I'd been wrong.

No one could ever be prepared enough for the waiting because I was never sure what I waited for would come.

Another day, another glorious day, but without human companionship I looked to creatures for comfort. Though they could be wondrous, there was so much to be missed by the human glance, the words, the smile, the touch. Yet this was why I did it, wasn't it? All of us in Tee-Pod were spirits who loved the world and humanity.

Carmella blinked, scampered toward me, and ran onto my hand and up my arm, finally resting on my shoulder. I rubbed the top of her head. When the coddling stopped, she leaned in for more.

It was Tuesday afternoon and the sun beamed hot. *Would one come today?*

No one came. They never did. One hundred eighty seven Tuesdays and still no one came. I plucked her from my shoulder, carried her back down the knoll, into the hillhouse, and set her upon the floor. She scratched at the hard dirt wall to sharpen her claws as I finished preparing dinner. I was good at dinners.

~ ~ ~

The floral bouquet I gathered of spring dandelions and violets would prove tasty as a side salad this eve. The rabbit stew had cooked all day and the meat was so soft it had fallen apart into thin strips in the clay pot. The only way I liked my rabbit was tender and stringy.

The smell couldn't help but force me to remember my first hunting experience in this new land. Even though the little hoppers were abundant, it still took me two days to catch one, once I finally set it in my head to. After practice, I could snare a rabbit in fifteen minutes.

Still, I preferred chicken meat to rabbit. Chickens were easier to catch, but rarely seen. They hid, so squirrels were what I ate most. The one thing I disliked about making squirrel was those tiny bones. Trying to get the meat off them if you cooked it whole was like shelling crab for its precious meat at the eating room back home. The best thing about squirrel was that they weren't scarce, and tasted better than rabbit. Even at that they evaded me this morning, so it was rabbit I found myself eating tonight.

I removed the flora from the counter and began plucking the pieces from the stalks. I used only the leaves from the dandelions and the petals of the violets, then threw the scraps out the door for the rabbits to pick at. Slipping the new wooden plate from the old one beneath, I uncovered the other herbs and checked them for moistness. The parsley and basil were damp enough to enjoy fully. Putting a few large pieces of each into the salad, I reached for the hanging leather bag near the window and added several drops of apple vinegar. Carmella was on the table waiting for me. I threw her a strip of rabbit meat which she engulfed in a quick moment and then I sat down to eat.

Once again I wondered who they would be sending and when he would get here. My mind was patient, but my heart grew anxious. Had Tarron really told me it would be a year or two, or had it been so long I'd forgotten? Living alone, I suppose I'd forgotten some things about humanity, but in all certainty they said a year or two. Either they were mistaken, or he was late.

I hoped I would remember social skills when he got here. Worried about communication, I'd kept up with my languages by speaking to Carmella in each of them throughout my day. I wondered which language he would speak. Which pod would he come from, Tee-Pod, Crue-Pod, or one of the others? I did my part. Where was he?

It crossed my mind that father couldn't fix the machine, but of course he would fix it. Aside from being head of the science division, he was a Seer too, after all. He would view the Pool and know I was here alone. He would never tolerate that. Perhaps the Earth had already died. What if no one ever came? I was so tired of being alone.

I was special, Tarron had said, *special.* My genes were perfect for travel, I had a photographic memory and my IQ was among the highest in the pods. From a group of a thousand I was picked to be the first through, the healthiest child of the Tee-Pod Community, genetically the strongest.

My chance of surviving travel was the greatest, they'd said. Ironic as it was, for all the studying and training, the swim turned out to be simple for me. It was nothing more than stepping through the wet puddle, feeling a blast of bright light burning at my closed eyes, then a moment of walking in a dream. Finally, there'd been a feeling as if a hard smack to the back from a wide board, and then it was done. I rolled into the grasses and here I was on this hillside. The others did not survive.

Before we swam, Tarron said another would be sent through a year or two later, a male, for physical strength. He'd said, "Wait and do not wander from the place."

Carmella climbed up to the edge of the shallow bowl and helped herself to more rabbit string. I picked up a violet petal and let it melt on my tongue. Sixteen, now.

"Happy birthday," I said, then swallowed it down.

Chapter Three

Kenter sat on the edge of his rack in Tee-Pod Three's Elite Sleeve. Sweat tickled the side of his forehead. He palmed it away. Today's workout was short. There was studying to do. Yes, he had researched and practiced the early ways of electricity, but he needed to refresh his mind one last time. He revisited the written material daily, and today would be no exception. He also practiced the exhausting task of using paper and pen, though he hated writing without his Mindline. The ink took too long to settle on the thin, fibrous material.

His thoughts ran to Professor Maxy. The prof was such a hard nose today in class. Maxy never let up on Kenter, constantly berating his efforts with questions he was sure the candidate had no answers for, subjects like whistle weed and wound sap, things that were irrelevant. Still, what an honor for Maxy to have selected him to go first.

Kenter was running out of patience in his urgency to leave. Without a doubt, the clean world was where he belonged. He'd felt this way since he could remember. In his dreams, the clean world offered a great warmth that nothing here, not even his sister's love, could equal. Those dreams felt more real than the pods ever had.

He stripped off his clothes and stepped into the shower to wash off his workout, resenting the fact his physical strength had been blown into a major issue, into such a large part of this deal. The news spewed the fact that part of his *training* was body building. He was a brainiac and didn't much care for candidates' required weight lifting or physical endurance exercises. None the less, the workouts had molded him quite nicely into a more muscular male, as if he needed more attention from the overly eager females.

As the water ran down his face, he wondered if any of the Originals would be waiting when he arrived. Had they survived?

Kenter himself was tired of waiting. He wanted to be there already.

Three decades had passed, almost to the day, since the first five candidates left the community and the machine failed during their swim. Twenty five years after the catastrophe, the Vision Fold re-established the Pool of Light Project. Kenter waited, his years of training, for the light point portal to reopen. He was getting older by the minute. This was his only chance for a launch. With any delay, when the next swim occurred he could be sterilized and refused, due to age. He wouldn't let that happen. He *had* to go this swim.

After being denied admission into the academy the first time, to give way to those much younger candidates, he had pursued his goal with vengeance, finally accepted because of his sister's idea. Still, he deserved it and had worked hard to ensure nothing would get in his way. Next week, he would swim and create the path for the future of mankind.

Kenter secretly hoped the Originals had not survived. Not because he wished them harm, of course, but something about being *The First* was more important to him than anything else. He wanted to be the one to survive and stake claim to the first settlement. Then he would be the oldest, the elder. He wanted to matter that much in the clean world. Being one of them was not enough. He was meant to be *The First*.

~ ~ ~

Arden was waiting by the eating room door when Kenter arrived.

"Are you ever on time?" his best friend asked.

Kenter's glance was brief before he walked to the tray crate and pulled out a yellow tray. Then he stepped up to the non-existent line beneath the gold sign that read '*Elite Menu.*' He selected vegetable soup with bits of actual and delectable roasted beast cooked into it as his main dish. The pieces were enormous, the size of the nail on his pinky finger. He wondered where they'd found a beast big enough to offer chunks of meat this size. Their delicious look made his mouth water as he watched the server ladle soup into the bowl. He selected fresh dwarf strawberries with real sugar cane as dessert, before strutting across the room and sliding into the chair beside Arden. His friend seemed clingier than usual today.

"Nervous yet?" Arden asked.

"About?" Kenter replied arrogantly.

"Yeah, right." Arden rolled his eyes. "You're smooth as glass."

Kenter *was* nervous and more anxious than he would ever let on, even to Arden. His being first to step into the Pool of Light would make and change the future. He was the main character and in the limelight at the pods. Nothing bigger existed, here or on the other side. He was oldest at training camp, the most educated. Everyone knew it. Everyone accepted it.

Elated he'd out-tested Lethia on this morning's math exam, he began spooning the huge pieces of beast and vegetables bits into his mouth. The great smell and taste of it took his mind elsewhere, until his friend interrupted.

"Belle says Sandra's upset," said Arden.

"Like I care, Ard," replied Kenter.

"She says you've been ignoring her… more than usual," Arden continued.

"I don't have time for her and her father's games," said Kenter.

Arden stared at the beautiful female in the distance who stood in the green serving line. He licked his lips. Her long hair rested midway down her back. The candidate's required slacks couldn't hide the fact her legs took up more than half of her body. She watched Kenter as a server spooned food onto her green tray.

"She's viewing you," said Arden.

Arden was ridiculous. The fact that Sandra Lockley was the prettiest female at the academy infatuated the guy. Appearance-wise, Sandra was the enticement of perfection, yes, but Kenter knew better than to let that move him. He'd found her to be self centered and dense in the mind, plus she had an ulterior motive in all she did. She thought of herself as a master manipulator and deceiver, but her intentions were obvious to him.

His friend seemed to care little for the fact that Sandra's father, Senator Lockley, had it in for Kenter. The senator made repeated attempts to thwart his impending swim. Irritation rolled through Kenter. How could Arden put thoughts of females before all else, including training and swims?

"Gravity, don't wait until Tuesday," he said to Arden, whose eyes remained fixated on the green line. "Your grades are enough. The board will approve you for a date with her," replied Kenter. "I told you before, one date was one too many. I know you want to submit. It won't bother me. Actually, you'd be doing me a gift. Perhaps then she'll leave me alone."

Arden raised his brows and crinkled his face into a deliberate mocking motion. Whatever he tried to resemble, he failed miserably.

"Be serious for once," Kenter continued, talking through a mouthful of soup. "I don't have time for goggle-headed females pondering love. Just submit the council paperwork and take her out. But don't blow your slot over her. Double up on your shots. She's mad as they get and she'll try to put you in the bad light if you're not cautious. Well, a worse light than you're already in, anyway. I know you won't listen, but try."

"I mean, view her," said Arden, ignoring his friend's advice completely. "Kenter, she's dropped her fork. She's bending down. Quick! View her! You won't fall over dead. Those legs."

Kenter did not turn to see, but rather stomped his friends foot.

"Your logic's idiotic," he said, shaking his head. "I'm swimming in less than a week."

"I'd be using that to my advantage," replied Arden. "She told Claire she'd show you her thighs if you asked. It'd be well worth the risk, and they won't boot you from a swim this close to launch for viewing thighs. Besides, who knows how long it'll be before your eye's will see another female's face, let alone a set of legs?"

"You know what she tried to do. She hasn't even crossed my mind," answered Kenter.

Kenter took a deep breath before asking his question.

"Speaking of eyes, what were you and Mize talking about in his office?"

"When?" said Arden.

"This morning," Kenter knew Arden was simply guising himself as a fool.

"Did Leth see me?" Arden replied, as if surprised.

If anyone was good at a guise, it was Arden.

"Come on... spit it. You knew she'd speak it to me. It's not like a punitive meeting with Mize has ever stayed unnoticed," Kenter scolded. "What'd you do this time?"

He waited through the long pause, before his friend answered.

"They moved me down the list," Arden replied, scratching at his nose.

Kenter stopped chewing and huffed.

"Again?" he said under his breath. "How far down?"

"One hundred twenty."

Kenter shot a furious glare to his friend.

"Miser from the sulfur pits, Arden," he whispered his curse through gritted teeth. "That's almost a *year* pushed back. A couple more times, you won't go at all. If you don't stop ogling females, you'll *never* swim. Where are your priorities? Can't you keep your eyes on studying, training, reading... important things? You'd place a female's biology before your own swim?"

Arden smirked. He couldn't help it. He was not like Kenter. His every breath did not revolve around a scheduled swim. Arden just wanted a mate. Too bad the one he preferred most was slotted to swim.

Arden thought the law of forcing candidates to wait until the age of twenty to match was ludicrous. He could be a fine mate to any one of a handful of females right now. He was sure of it. The feeling stirred in him whenever he viewed them.

Five-hundred milligrams of Testrophine per day did not seem enough lately to quash his growing desires. Besides, he didn't believe wholeheartedly the world was really to end, at least not anytime soon.

He and Lethia spoke secretly on the subject just two days ago. They wondered if the seers had really seen the end, or if it was simply speculation. After all, everyone had heard the story since they could remember, yet nothing was any worse or better than before.

The only real scare had been the other pod's solar fire two years ago, which wiped out a large percentage of those citizens as well as one of their candidates, but those flares never touched Tee-Pod's community. The only devastation Tee-Pod felt in recent times was the library fire, which occurred over a decade ago, when he was just a child. Sometimes he wondered if there was real danger of world destruction, or if it was the pod council's way of controlling the people.

He waited to ignore the lecture he was sure he'd get from his best friend about this morning's punitive session with the head of the science division, Senator General Mize Maxy himself.

"I will never understand what goes through your mind," Kenter continued. "If you can't handle the temptation, get a shot of Testestronine to head it off, before the council ends your candidacy all together. I mean... you're mad as a storm meter. At this rate, you'll be sterilized before you get a chance to leave. You've got twenty-years-old coming in two years. Are you trying to be stuck here?"

Arden shrugged.

"You can't afford another mess up, Ard."

Kenter's friend scanned the room to ensure no one was watching, before he swiped a strawberry from the plate, and promptly popped it onto his awaiting tongue. His brow took on a sudden serious expression.

"It won't be the same here when you go, Kent."

"Yeah. Who will keep your head clear?" answered Kenter. "And give you strawberries?"

Kenter's frustration with Arden aside, he would miss him greatly. They met their first year of training and he'd never known a more loyal friend. No one in the pod community cared less for rules than Arden, but he was entertaining and the most fun to be around.

When they initially met, Kenter had been leery of befriending him, afraid that the jokester's blatant disregard for seriousness could potentially cause problems for him as well, or worse yet, that the professors would think poorly of Kenter because of his choice of a rule bending friend. But, as it turned out, their personalities balanced out one another and the instructors tolerated Arden's distractions, for regardless of his diminishing ranking on the swim schedule, Arden remained a top student. He was one of the brightest in the academy and had, on occasion, out-tested even Kenter and Lethia.

Kenter knuckled his friend's shoulder, but held back his words about missing him. He could not be portrayed as weak. Any small sign of weakness would be noticed. Even at this late stage in the game he worried the council would change its mind, choose another candidate to go in his stead.

He wouldn't risk it, so he said not a word to Arden about missing anyone at the pods. A momentary glance of acknowledgement said it all. That was the extent of the verbal exchange. Arden knew what it meant. Kenter would miss him, too.

He could read Kenter better than anyone, other than Lethia.

Tolomay's World and The Pool of Light

Chapter Four

Lethia brushed her long hair before she swept it up and wrapped it into a tight ponytail. As she slipped on her workout attire, she thought on this morning's final math exam. Her brother had won. She would be taking his task at wiping down the walls until the swim, because of it.

Studying the smooth white corners in the room, she wondered how replicating these multiple walls would be possible without the advantage of proper tools. She had been practicing with sharp rocks and wooden peg nails and gears, as instructed, but it proved difficult. Her work took much longer than she'd expected. The results she offered this morning appeared meager in comparison to the building she now stood within. This one, of course, had been constructed with the pod's modern tools. Still, it was obvious why she was not allowed the use of them for the exam.

What would she actually have available to her on the other side, when the time came to create the community's multi-sided gowas? If construction was done well, and the shapes formed perfectly, the extra time with archaic tools would be more than worth the effort, she decided.

A Carpentry Architecture expert to the core, Lethia was well versed in the importance of the properly constructed sacred gowas, which the community residents lived within. They afforded greater spaces in rooms than any other style of home building. Abodes built in this manner, not only offered the greatest views and use of natural lighting and heating, but also provided safety from many things. That would be important.

These walls which stood before her, these great, smooth, white walls, with their paint reflecting the lighting to every inch of the room, were something she appreciated in their entirety.

She enjoyed knowing each step involved in the building of their homes. Even the metal plates welded to the outer walls, to protect pod residents from the horrific sun, had been designed perfectly. Their look didn't bother her, and she was sure most residents didn't even notice them. After all, they had been painted over numerous times. For years, the focus of Lethia's studies had been on important details such as this.

She remembered Professor Manngie's first words to her about ancient geometry.

"It is behind all proper structures ever built, and the key to the entirety of the world."

Lethia learned that ancient geometry was the basic design for life itself. She was grateful to have been assigned Michael Manngie and Mize Maxy as her professors. They were, after all, the finest and most knowledgeable in the pod community.

Her training, which was identical to those used by the greatest architects of all time, would help her draw and construct the building she would soon be overseeing.

Pod tales told that the ancient's cities of Athens, Jerusalem, Egypt and some Aztec structures based on those same architectural methods, had even survived the annihilations of the weather wars. Of course the people in those communities hadn't survived, and truly, the rest of the tale was speculation, but Lethia chose to believe those structures still remained today.

As she viewed the ceiling joints, she felt Tee-Pod's gowas were even stronger than those of the ancients. They had been perfected to the fullest by implementing nature's example into ancient knowledge. Her community was one of the few still intact because of their construction.

Each community gowa boasted eight sides and eight corners and nestled together like octagonal bee-hives representing perfect communities. While bee-hives kept only six sides, eight sided structures proved most efficient to house a room's furniture. They also created more floor space for citizens to move about. Plus, they were aesthetically pleasing. She loved that. Lethia enjoyed immaculate construction and sterile appearance. She wanted things to look as perfect as the math they were based upon.

If time math were as linear and easily

learned, she would have beaten Kenter's score on this morning's test. She could never figure time math, no matter her efforts. Still, after today it no longer mattered. He won their bet. She would do her brother's work until the launch.

Oh well, at the least of it, his higher score made him feel more sure of himself. In that, she was glad he had won, though she had tried.

She rubbed her long slender fingers over the crack in the wall. These past years, the growing line that started at the floor had slowly worked its way upward. Since she began marking it, it nearly doubled in length, the tip now almost as tall as her. Even in its perfection, according to the seers, this place would soon become a pile of dust. How much longer would the strong surrounding walls protect her community from the environment?

The Science Advisors recently broadcasted the doom and gloom weather on the news. They reported to the entire community, saying it was only a matter of months before the pod walls would begin to fettle, which was the term used to describe a structure's serious disintegration due to solar storm wear and tear. After the announcement, Mize took her and Kenter aside, to tell them the truth of the matter.

He disclosed that those reported *months*, would actually total around *five years* if the weather did not worsen, less time if it did. Mize felt the two needed to know why the council exaggerated the truth in a manner so blatantly overstated; it could be construed as a lie to the entire community. Then, he shared a great secret. The Science Advisors of the council had each agreed to the illegal act of lying in order to protect humanity as a whole. No adult ever mentioned anything so shocking to Kenter or Lethia as that confession. Those brilliant scientists had deliberately lied. Who would think it?

While Mize's trust and information took them by surprise, one thing was clear. The weather situation was very serious, and the elders protesting the use of the Pool of Light needed their voices squashed. Humanity *did* need protecting, and Mize's team had stepped up to the plate to do just that. Lethia could not think it how a citizen would go against a swim, but some had. They were most often the lesser educated elders, paranoid a radiation leak from the Pool of Light would kill the entire pod.

But the Science Division knew better. Over and over, they tested the machine. What happened to the first candidates, the *Originals*, could never happen again. It would be impossible. The time scars were healed. The Science Division repaired the device and plugged all the holes. It was perfectly safe, for both candidates and pod citizens.

Aside from the legal end, Lethia and Kenter were grateful the Science Division's exaggeration worked to quiet those against the launch. For no young candidate could risk anything halting the swims they waited for and trained so long to make.

Lethia thought to the Originals. Had the Pool of Light incinerated them as most believed? If it hadn't, surely the professors would have taught the students something of those citizens. Since words of the dead were not to be spoken, in all certainty they *must* be dead.

If they had survived, day to day life in the clean world would be much different than in the pods. Daily words of the upcoming catastrophe would not be looming constantly in the air in the clean world as it did here.

Mankind was nearing its end at the pods. In a handful of years all animal and human life would cease to exist. No one could stop it from happening. It had been foreseen in the machine and so was set in unbendable time. All living things would simply perish from the Earth in one horrific event. Seers had viewed it in the Pool of Light for decades, debating the community's choices at each annual session.

Science Division Seers determined before the first swim, that it would take a thousand years for the world to renew itself. That much time was needed until humanity and other multi-celled creatures would once again benefit from the graces of the Earth in order to survive. The planet had protected herself over the last half century, harbored her energy, and starved living things in order to do so. Her current focus was the last of humankind, and rightfully so. For no creature had ruined Earth more than the hands of ancient man. It furried Lethia to think it. How selfish the ancients had been to her generation and the future of all people.

If the swims failed, the only beasts in Earth's future in a thousand years would be amoebas, and any other single celled organism that could be viewed beneath the lens of a microscope. Man, would simply perish forever.

Those who fought against the Vision Fold's *Pool of Light* project were heartless. They seemed to Lethia as the crazed ancients, though she would never compare them to, nor use the term GoldHorder about anyone. No one alive could be as evil as that group had been.

She could only guess why some of the older citizens opposed the Light swims. Was it because they were too old to travel? No matter what happened with the Vision Fold Project, the elders were guaranteed certain death on this ruined Earth.

How could any be so selfish to think it should be allowed for human life to die off, simply because they would? Tribe teachings advised toward survival of humanity in the future of the Earth, after all. Something seemed very wrong with those handful of older ones who lacked community mind, and always seemed petrified of the coming doom. They were too solitary.

Only a bit nervous of the world's end, Lethia was never terrified of it, not really. Shy, yes, compliant, yes, quiet, in all certainty, but terrified of the world's end? No.

Her generation was told the end story so many times since birth that it barely phased them to think it. Besides, in some way it seemed unreal that it would actually happen. After all, it was not here now in front of them looking them right in the face. Unlike the elders, no one within her age group remembered a time without quakes and storms, or when constant talk of the end of the livable Earth did not exist.

To the youth of the community things seemed just as normal as ever. The only time she worried was when seeing the fear in those elder's eyes. It unnerved her, and so she steered clear of them. Her focus must remain on the future, the clean world, and her building skills.

Her eyes scanned the room. While the only lighting afforded here was artificial, knowing she would soon create spaces that used natural sunlight elated her. It would brush itself onto the walls without any form of generator. What a glorious sight that would be.

Surely sunlight was breathtaking, but would it be truly safe there? Would it burn at their skin or eyes during extended exposure as they had been taught? Hopefully, training was correct and a tree's shade *would* bring enough shelter so the sun would not prove fatal. She knew without a doubt being cooked by a solar flare was the most horrid way to die. She heard told the stories about the fallen pods.

Lethia wiped the worry from her mind, pulled on her shoes and quickly tied the strappings. Her eyes caught sight of the octagonal mobile hanging at the far corner of the ceiling and smiled. It was a small dream-catcher her brother made for her with three real ancient feathers lining its bottom.

The dust they carried, forced a sneeze from her as she removed it from the hanger to rub her fingers across the stiff hair-like protrusions on their ends. Of course the feathers were old and tattered, but their hard center stems remained straight and intact. They were as the pictures she'd seen of fish skeletons, but soft fibers remained at their tips. When she felt their ends, it comforted her.

Kenter never did tell her where he found the priceless treasures, no matter how many times she asked. She guessed it was Arden's doing. He never feared broken rules as Kenter and Lethia did. Perhaps he swiped them from one of the science labs, not that she cared where they came from.

Far from being a rule breaker, she normally would have cared. But this close to the swim it no longer bothered her. Besides, they mesmerized her as they hung from the edge of the dream-catcher. She'd never received a more precious gift. She was fortunate enough to have a sibling at all, but felt grateful in the truest sense to have a brother to love her who was as protective and loving as Kenter.

On one side of the coin, he was her rock, and on the flipside, she offered *him* protection against himself. He was stubborn to a great fault.

She sneezed again, then rubbed the dust from the delicate item onto her garment, until satisfied it was clean.

Quite sure the council would

confiscate it if they knew she owned it, Lethia never reported this gift, as was required. It was not as if she had months to enjoy it.

She felt no one could truly blame her for the crime of illegal feathers, for she played no part in the getting of them. But it was best not to take chances even this close to the launch. Besides, feathers weren't needed for hunting anymore. Citizens hadn't been allowed outside for decades. Even if they had, there was nothing left alive to hunt.

After the bees and fish disappeared, birds were one of the next species to become extinct. Feathers for bows were impossible to find after that, so it became forbidden for anyone but the pod council to own them. The law against owning feathers, though old, had never been removed from the papers. Even Mize had seen the mobile and done nothing.

She hadn't been too worried about Kenter's gift at the time. In all certainty she was due a rule bend or two. Always the reserved intellect, she violated just two rules in the entirety of her life. Only one citizen knew, and that citizen would never speak it either.

Not even Kenter knew. He was the

last person she would confide in because he would react with his stubborn, blown out tongue. His worrying for it would pain her ears until the launch. She decided never to tell him. Stolen time alone with another, holding hands for a moment, and those two kisses had been the riskiest thing she'd ever done. She'd chosen to do it twice, yet still couldn't believe she had done it at all. It was as if another body took over hers for a moment, and then was returned, wide eyed and remorseful.

Well, as remorseful as one can be after feeling the pleasure of nature's lips to another. But yes, some things a sister doesn't tell a brother, especially when the brother is slotted as the first male to swim and the lips belong to their friend.

Lethia was famous for being the most cooperative candidate. She had received public recognition for it. Until those kisses, she had always followed rules. So when Mize came to her room seven days ago, he merely glanced at the mobile, winked and smiled, and said nothing about the feathers. He knew Lethia. She would not well survive the public lecture that would occur, were she caught with an unreported gift.

Only when called to the council room mere hours later, did she fear it had been reported. Her heart raced with worry until the inquisition presented its questions. They weren't about her at all, but rather Kenter's hearing.

She was not surprised to find the investigation initiated by Senator Lockley. He'd been trying to keep Kenter from this swim for the past three years, and Lethia's idea had caused it.

Lockley's daughter, Sandra, was bumped from first on the list to swim, down to third place. It was all Lethia's doing. She designed an idea that gave Kenter the possibility to swim. Sandra's declining test scores since that day had pushed her name down further, to where she now stood at number nine. Her father was not happy.

Why did Lockley continue to punish Kenter because of Sandra's failings? It would not bring his daughter back to the top. Lethia couldn't help the upward turn of her lips as she remembered that day. Perhaps Lockley wasn't really targeting her brother. Maybe he was simply eager to rid himself of his daughter. She had never cared for

Sandra.

Pushing her memories aside, she rubbed gently at the knots that kept the mobile's shape in place, and once again thought to the safety of her brother. While sure she could control the building of structures, her brother's well-being and his swim through time was another matter entirely. Would science and chance be enough to keep him alive?

Females scored higher in every single test regarding the Pool of Light. It was fact. Would he survive the passage? She couldn't help but worry, even if there was no logic in it. She knew what going meant to him: everything. It was all he talked about in his youth, even before they re-opened the academy. He dreamed about being the first through since he could speak.

Kenter had never been happier than she'd seen him these past years while training with the Vision Fold Project. Even *her* love toward the clean world was dwarfed by his passion to go.

Her brother was fulfilling his life's dream and dedicated in doing so. She would be supportive of him, to any and every extent possible. Telling him her concerns for his safety regarding his swim was something she would never bring herself to do. He'd logic she was questioning his competence. It could affect his confidence level. It could break his mindset during transport, throw him off mentally.

As proud as he was, he was still male, and egos can grow weak in the presence of unwelcomed words. He needed to remain strong in every area. Nothing must divert his concentration if he was to survive the swim. More than that though, Lethia knew how capable Kenter was of contributing greatly to the clean world. She loved her brother and knew his many strengths, even if humility wasn't one of them. He had to survive, for the good of the community. There was that, and she could not bear the thought of life without him.

~ ~ ~

The subtle smell of mint invaded her nostrils when Lethia walked through the entry door into the gym lab. She threw her towel on the rack, disappointed to see Delores today, equipment in hand, ready and waiting for her. This female would have heard the news of Arden's meeting with Mize by now. She was so talkative. Though it was against pod rules, she spread words eagerly, more so than anyone Lethia knew.

Delores enjoyed stirring pots, ruffling up doubt regarding others, but was exempt from punishment for it, likely because she was matched with the son of a senator commander. The female was arrogant and irritating. Lethia could only just tolerate her.

Today, Delores's breath smelled strongly of mint tea. She exaggerated her words and breathed out the heavy scent, seemingly to make Lethia envious. Even the elite candidates were not allowed it. Mints were reserved for specific council meetings.

Lethia wished she had the luxury of that tea, but no matter. Soon enough she would have access to more mint than she could ever hope to drink. How was it this trainer always found her way to the forbidden, and no one said or did a thing for it?

At least the teacup offered Delores warm hands. Lethia was grateful for that. The trainer's fingers were not cold as she scanned Lethia's heart, and stuck the sticky monitors on her forehead, down the length of her chest and onto the arch of her back. She pushed a few buttons and sat to view the health screen.

The workout machine switched itself on when Lethia positioned herself on the rower seat. She began thrusting through the faux rapids that showed on the video screen before her.

"So... mouths have it Arden has done it again," said Delores.

"Mmm?" replied Lethia, pretending not to hear or care.

"Apparently, the male has no eye control at all, another meeting with Mize. If he's not careful, they'll strike him from the program," Delores continued.

This female was so cruel. Lethia's heart raced.

"No one has told me they've seen him touch a female, Delores. Have you heard differently?"

"Not yet, but it's simply a matter of time. From what I've heard, it seems he has little to no respect for mating and celibacy laws. Perhaps he isn't complying with his required five-hundred milligrams."

Lethia didn't answer. Arden did comply with hormone laws and he was still an innocent, like all other candidates and anyone before the age of twenty. He was none of Delores's business. He'd never breeched celibacy rules. He would have told her.

What did Delores care anyway? At seven years past twenty, she was too old for a swim. That was what bothered her. Arden was just show of it. He wouldn't actually break *that* law, would he?

Lethia knew him well. He confided his true nature to her often, when Kenter wasn't present. Regardless of his joking talk, and his somewhat wandering eyes, he desperately wanted to swim. The problem was he also wanted a match. Who could blame one with no parent or sibling for wanting a life match? She and Kenter and other siblings in the community had an advantage. Life was lonelier for the rest.

Lethia stared the female's eyes away. If Delores knew the truth of it, she would have realized community members spoke much more often of the med trainer's loose mouth than they did of Arden's loose eyes. If Delores knew that, perhaps the busy tongued female would stop digging around and spreading nonsense.

"Kenter should be more cautious in selecting his friends," Delores continued.

"He is leaving, Delores. Kenter's eyes concern themselves only with training and he's more than prepared for this swim. What he and his friends do is none of anyone else's concern," said Lethia, who was growing angrier with each strained breath.

Lethia decided against pursuing the argument. She realized what was truly upsetting her was the stress building about the swim, more so than her trainer's words. It was unlike her to meet argument with another. Lethia was peace loving. This cheating female was not worth an emotional spar. Instead, she eyeballed Delores as she drew in her next deep breath and pulled the rower's handles nearer to her chest. She would simply change the subject, but the trainer spoke before she could.

"What's wrong?" Delores asked.

"A little concerned about safety," Lethia answered.

"They've tested the machine a hundred times this week. The holes are gone," remarked Delores.

"I know," replied Lethia.

"So, what then?" asked Delores. "Is

he still giving you grief about the council questioning you?"

Now she'd done it. This female had insulted both Arden and Kenter. Why would she choose it?

"No," Lethia answered protectively. "Just worried about him."

"So he finally forgave you then?" Delores continued on. "It wasn't as if you had a choice in answering the council's call for questions. What is wrong with him? Why he worried himself sick they were going to change their mind because of a hearing test... ha, it's beyond me. After all, he scored in the ninety eight percentile."

"It wasn't a hundred percent," defended Lethia. "My brother felt good reason for concern."

"Oh, for gravity's sake," said Delores, with brows raised.

She shook her head at Lethia.

"So he finally found out he wasn't perfect," continued Delores. "Who knew?"

"Off," Lethia said through gritted teeth. Her clenched jaw was partially due to strain of rowing, and partially from frustration.

Delores responded to Lethia's command by hitting a red button on her health screen. She stared.

"Something else holds your thoughts today. Something besides your brother," she insisted.

It was not a question Lethia would answer. She wondered about the Originals who'd first gone through the pool. So much time had passed since then. If they *had* survived the swim, would they have survived the environment? Would they be there alone?

The monitor beeped three times, then the sound of gears ceased. The screen of flowing rapids shut off. Delores removed the sticky strips from Lethia's body as soon as she stood.

"I'll do the run alone today," Lethia said, clearly frustrated at her trainer.

"Keep quiet then," Delores responded. "None of my business anyway, Leth," she finished, and Lethia began her lone jog around the room.

Tolomay's World and The Pool of Light

ChapTer Five

The old, dry branches I set outside the window last night were broken this morn. It was the bear again. Not that I didn't love the living creatures here, but that stupid bear was quite another thing. He ruined my property and stole food. He broke my first oven, the one that took weeks to build and ran off with my smoked meat and rabbit blanket; though, I did not know what he could possibly have needed with a blanket.

Why can't bears be vegetarians? He was rotten and I despised him. He was cute to view when a cub, but now that he'd grown a bit, all he did was harass me several times a year for weeks on end, then disappear until the next haunt.

Oh well, at least I was safe. It was good that Tarron prepared me for these things. Otherwise, I would not have known to construct windows using existing trees to keep that furry menace out. I looked more closely at one of the tree trunks supporting the wall. Bear claw marks. How did I sleep through that?

Marking my house as his territory... humph, what a pest. It must be the raspberries. That's what he was after last time, too.

"Those dark ones from on top of the hill, remember Carmella?"

Carmella skittered into the kitchen and climbed up the cabinet in record time, then greeted me at the window. I was still examining the outer structure. There were no dents in the wall beneath the grass. It held.

"We'll have to try the water hemlock raspberry mix again. Maybe he'll eat the poison this time." I said to the uninterested lizard.

"I'll have to cage you again for a few days, honey."

Carmella nearly fell off the edge of the sill, chasing after a bug that was faster than her tongue.

Sorry, Tarron. I know you wouldn't approve of killing a creature other than for food, but I just can't have this bear in my world. He's crazy. I'll keep a pot on the fire and scald him with boiling water the next time he comes at night. I'll throw it out the window.

"That's what we'll do, Carmella. That'll teach him to mark our home."

Hungry for breakfast, I swept Carmella from the sill and carried her inside. Precious goose eggs were on the menu.

It grated at me while I ate. There were only two things that scared me in this place. The cougars and that stupid bear, but the cougars seem more afraid of me than I am of them. That bear is afraid of nothing. I could have done just fine here without him, thank you very much. I loved the other animals, but why did the Vision Fold have to send bears? What were they good for anyway?

Would someone come soon? I did not even want to think what it would be like if the female reproduced again. Bears would be running amuck. I'd have no choice but to find a way to kill them, then. It would be much to handle alone.

I'd feel safer if Tarron's hunting armory had surfaced, but thus far I had no luck. If the others had survived we'd have found it together by now. There were defense weapons hidden there. I was sure of it.

"I have you though, don't I, sweetie?"

When I untied the chirping cricket sack and threw her a live one, she scarfed it down in one gulp, then skittered under my bedding and made herself comfortable. She settled there for the rest of the morning.

The clouds crawled in and stayed their wings. It rained all day. I washed up inside, rather than bathing in the stream. After this morning, I didn't want to risk running into the bear. He usually slept mornings on days he came menacing. But I could never be too sure when he would rear his ugly head on days like this morn. Above all else, I'd learned to practice safety where he was concerned.

~ ~ ~

I finished the new floor mat for the room and spread it out from the center to the edges. It lay flat enough. There was one lumpy area, but that would matt down within a few days. It smelled like fresh hay in the room and reminded me of the wheat room back home.

It was Monday. I hoped it wouldn't rain tomorrow. Carmella didn't enjoy the rain like I thought something so closely resembling a salamander should. She actually seemed to despise it. So when it rained on Tuesdays, I had to walk to the hill and wait alone. As absurd as it sounded, I was more comforted when she was with me, mostly during the few weeks a year the bear showed himself. While I was sure a lizard couldn't protect me from a bear, there was still something quite reassuring about knowing, or at least hoping, there was a living creature nearby who cared for me.

I had passion for this place, this clean world, but on days like today I grew a bit weak in spirit. I knew it was simple loneliness, but I always seemed to feel it more when that pesky bear came calling. Now, for some reason, he'd marked my house as his own. Stupid creature!

Please send him tomorrow, Tarron, a male for physical strength. Where was he?

I peered out into the night three times before I untied the skins and let them drape over the window. I did not hear him. The bear wasn't out there. With cloud cover tonight it was pitch black already and I was tired from the wet day. Carmella lay sprawled next to me on the bedding, all four bumpy legs stretched out. She was a scrawny little thing.

"Tomorrow's Tuesday," I said, as I blew out the flame of the clay lamp and closed my eyes.

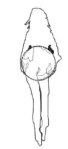

Chapter Six

Kenter stood in front of the mirror, smoothing the precious black silk-like fabric that hung on him. He tugged at the thin waist strap. Perfect. He was ready. Nausea rushed to his belly. *Was* he ready? Suddenly he did not feel particularly ready.

Though he hadn't been allowed breakfast, he felt as though he had eaten. His stomach was in knots and a wild food party was going on inside him, replete with dancing.

Adrenalin rushed through his veins. The ceremony hadn't yet started. He hadn't even left his room. How could he feel this ill at ease already? His feet screamed their tingles. He was too excited and making himself ill. It would not behoove him to show his nervousness on stage. He had to calm down.

But it was really happening. His dream was finally here. Today he would swim in the Pool of Light and make it to the other side, the first male to go. Standing here, he could almost taste its glory. People would speak of him for all eternity.

The knock on the door jolted him from his self centered day dream back to the here and now.

"Yeah," he said, slightly annoyed.

The door opened to Lethia's face. She donned a short dress that ended mid-thigh. Its black fabric matched Kenter's short pants and chest garb, though the attempt at covering his abdomen fell centimeters short of success.

She looked to his bare stomach. His top covered enough of him. It had been a wise choice. He would not need this garb in the clean world, and he looked smarter with longer hair... like an elder.

"Ready?" she asked.

"I was born for this," he answered in a cocky tone.

Lethia wasn't surprised at her brother's over confident answer. It was Kenter's standard reply to questions of this nature, questions that had anything remotely to do with ego.

"I talked to Professor Mirn and, Kenter, they've decided," she said with jubilation. "You can carry the Juper."

His face lit to an immense smile.

"He said to send it first," Lethia continued. "Just after you step through the first stage. It's safe. It won't blow a hole, but it may not go through all the way. Anyway, it's worth a try. They're entrusting it to you."

Kenter was elated. The Juper would prove a tremendous asset to the new community. He considered it to be his reward for having been top student.

Being the most precious of all things other than life itself, the Juper would help them to find the metals and glasses needed to construct anything mechanical in the clean world. Using it, he would be able to ease the burdens of their entire community and all would praise him. His name would be remembered, not only on this side, but in the clean world as well. His importance as *the first* would be known forever. He reveled in the satisfaction of it all.

~~~

His sister held his hand as they walked the corridor to the share-room.

Arden greeted them at the door with a hug. Kenter allowed this. After all, the council couldn't change launch candidates on the day of the swim. It was a sure thing at this point.

There was standing room only in the packed room. People stood elbow to elbow along the rear walls and behind those seated in the balcony. The space was overwhelmingly warm and well lit due to the array of news cameras and lights near the front podium.

Center stage boasted the transport pool area. Technically, it was an empty round pool, very shallow, with sides a mere six inches deep, but it was breathtakingly beautiful. Built with painstaking precision and made of copper and crystal tiles, it glistened in the vast light that poured in through cathedral skylights.

The back half of the pool was encased in a wall of solar panels that ran up to and through the colorful glass of the ceiling. Copper wires fastened into the main chasse. They glowed a bright florescent blue.

This was the first time since its initial use that the Pool of Light had been fully awakened. The council ordered removal of the heavy metal plates from the colorful roof to solar charge it. Kenter had never seen it fully prepared and was in awe of the magnificent sight, as was everyone in the room. His heart raced at the power of the moment. How many things had changed in the pod over the past five years!

Thirty years ago, after the last of Tolomay's group stepped through the Light, the power cell shorted out and radiated the fluid to hazardous levels. Citizens were outraged. They flew into a frenzy and demanded the project be shut down.

Council members met mass discontent and made the decision to terminate Vision Fold's project, thus condemning all hope for continued civilization in the process. Those decades ago, the council justified halting the project by saying it was a decision made to protect citizens from radioactivity.

Tarron Ramey, who birthed Vision Fold, felt it more of a political, rather than a humanitarian decision, one made by a corrupt office. He argued that the Vision Fold Project could be re-worked to prevent future hazards. An appeal was submitted to the Senator General's office, but before it was heard, Tarron died suddenly. His dream of a future clean world, one inhabited by humans, died with him.

Decades later when Tee-Pod's livable environment began diminishing five times more rapidly than expected, citizens once again grew concerned for humanity as a whole.

Mize Maxy replaced Senator General Martin and Tarron's decades old appeal was reconsidered. Until Maxy's term was granted, the council would hear nothing more about the use of the pool, but once elected, he and top science professors pleaded with council members.

They finally chose to see the logic in reinstating research teams to continue work on the Vision Fold dream, the dream to keep humankind alive by sending candidates into the future of the clean world.

The use of the Pool of Light was put to a vote before the majority. This time it unanimously passed. Preparations were set in motion to once again make it operational. What other choice did they have? Plants and animals that once flourished on Earth were dying off by the thousands.

Now, five years later, in one of the only remaining living communities in sector twenty, the Quantum pool was brought to life again, this time under much more stringent conditions.

Just feet away from the twins, Callety Moor stood beside Kenter and Lethia's professor, Senator General Mize Maxy. The twelve Tone Men stood in a single row behind them. A distance away to the left, two ancients held didgeridoos, prepared to play.

Kenter and his twin sister were hand in hand on the stage. Lethia smiled at her community. She would miss them all. Lethia and Kenter would make history today. Sister and brother would contribute to the stability and education of the community in the clean world. They would make the path for the others to follow. They would be heroes. Both candidates stood proudly waiting until Maxy finished his speech and shook their hands.

Callety handed Kenter the Juper and whispered something into his ear. Kenter gave Arden a last glance and a smile. He set his finger to his brow before turning to face the Pool of Light, his signal he would see Arden on the other side, once it was his turn to swim. Lethia was so afraid. Would they perish as the others before them?

She was to help her brother through the passage and would have to maintain a tight grip on him no matter all else, or he would be lost. Female energy of life was stronger than a male's. The womb of life played a large part of it.

That had been her thinking when she presented her idea to the council three years ago, and her theory had been proven scientifically sound. For, it was Lethia who had initially been selected to swim, not Kenter.

Not, that is, until she explained in great factual depth the biological bond between twins. She suggested her brother be tested to make the trip at her side. The council concurred with Maxy's decision to send Kenter along and his training began.

Lethia knew her brother was fortunate. She thought to the males without siblings. Even though they were needed for re-population, male candidates were initially banned from transport when the Vision Fold was re-established. Tarron designed the Pool of Light. He was the only science member who knew how to configure the mechanism for males to survive passage. But Tarron died.

When Maxy's team began tests on the repaired machine, every male who participated in the Vision Fold preliminaries was seriously injured, a few nearly killed. Some fell out even before making it through the first stage of liquid. The only one who passed the preliminaries was Kenter, and only because he was tested while holding his sister's hand.

Now, with Lethia's help, a male could safely travel through and into the clean world. Kenter should be safe as long as the two maintained physical contact. The tests confirmed it. Potential success of his passage was just under ninety five percent. That made his risks no higher than for any female.

Trembling like an infant, she clasped his hand firmly. He responded with an overly tight grip, though she felt him shiver as well. Covering his hand with her other, she trapped his one hand between both of hers. He held the all important Juper in his free hand, prepared to release it after the first stage of liquid. It was vital it went through. It would make things right for all of them. They would need its findings of buried items.

She gripped tighter, lest his sweating hand slip from hers. Kenter smiled confidently. He felt stronger that his sister was nervous. After all, he was the male, the protector. He had physical strength.

"Don't forget to close your eyes," he instructed, knowing blindness could occur if either forgot.

"I love you," she answered.

He loved her, too.

"See you on the other side," he said.

Kenter squeezed her hand and smiled. He was nervous, too, but much more excited than afraid. How fortunate for him to be meeting the destiny he'd waited his whole life for.

Above them, the noise of solar panels being repositioned sounded momentarily. The motion rattled the ceiling and walls, and then stopped abruptly. The ancients began playing their didgeridoos. The sound emanated from the instruments, filling the room and causing the hair on Kenter's arms to rise toward the ceiling. It was happening on his head, too, and it tingled. Kenter viewed Lethia whose hair was responding in much the same way; the ends and loose strands on top flipped upward. When she noticed his, her lips took an upward turn. The static electricity on the stage broke their tension.

The Didgeridoos' playing continued until the toners began to sing. The ancients set down their instruments, giving way for the singers to continue on, voice alone. A low baritone chord resonated from the group until together, as one voice, they slowly and steadily brought the pitch up, eventually resting on the chord Kenter and Lethia recognized. The familiar sound was that of ancient monastery meditations and had been required research for them both. They found the videos made eons ago on old box computers in the training pod. This was the proper key, the sound correct. They held each other's gaze. It was nearly time.

The chord was working. Excitement

filled the room as energy soared and brought the machine to life. All felt its presence. Maxy removed a glass urn. He began pouring the liquid from it into the empty pool at center stage. The fluid was a bright florescent blue before it settled to a deep, magical purple.

"Peace of life, my children," Maxy said to the two.

"Peace of life," the twins replied their answer.

These were the pod's spoken words of farewell and their cue to swim as well. Kenter closed his eyes tightly.

The room smelled of heated metals, as if something good was cooking. The faint noise of electricity sounded before him. Barely audible, it was masked by the music of the toners chorus. Still, he could hear its current running. His heart raced as if ready to leap from his chest.

He was in the heat of it as he stepped his first step. Adrenaline took charge of him until a wave of tingles settled upon his arms. It tortured him in a million relentless tickles, as if electricity itself danced on his skin. With one hand holding both of Lethia's, and the other wrapped firmly around the Juper, he could do nothing to rub the feeling away. Neither could she.

More frustrating, though, was that he couldn't step as fast as he'd like to, while walking blindly through the shallow liquid, holding her hand behind him. A surge of empowerment swept through him. He was overwhelmed as for one glorious moment, he remembered what awaited him on the other side of time. He monitored his breathing and pulled his sister's hands, quickly guiding her into the pool as his feet continued forward. He could hardly wait to get there.

"Breathe, Leth," he said, speaking as much to himself as he was to her.

Lethia gasped in her air. Eyes closed, she gripped his hand tighter and followed closely behind, until both candidates were splashing through the wet glowing fluid as one. Lightning flashed in the enormous room as the two disappeared from sight. In a mere instant, they were gone.

Tolomay's World and The Pool of Light

ChapTer Seven

A young male was tied to a piece of furniture in the room. The old male force fed his prisoner a spoonful of something from a metal container, then turned to the control panel before him. Directly above it, scenes played on a large screen. He pressed a button on the weather machine, forcing winds and water to sweep over citizens' individual homes on the video.

Their properties were blasted to bits. Grown males, females, and babies screamed for their lives while the water bombarded and pounded them. An infant wailed as a female was forced beneath the waves, losing her grip of the child. The old male at the controls laughed eerily.

I awoke in a sweat. Memories flooded back to me of the Pool of Light as it sucked the others into itself. My stomach was unsettled. Still, at the least of it, it was Tuesday.

I went outside to release my water and then returned to the hillhouse and began preparing breakfast. Carmella was nowhere to be seen.

Why had I dreamed about the ancients? Their destruction and attempt to exterminate each other was sickening. The manipulations, the One World government's conspiracy of selling secretly poisoned foods to the masses, in an attempt to kill off millions, were appalling. The weapons and wars over land and natural resources, weather machines destroying humans and animals in great numbers, all of it had been the greatest evils of mankind.

Attempts to leave the healthier pieces of the world untarnished for the few families of the GoldHoarders, the self-acclaimed "elite" of society, while others perished, had been the grandest stain of past society. They deliberately divided united peoples in order to create war to clear the population.

But today, none of Earth's past was a threat to me. History didn't affect me, or this place. The weapons and weather machines the GoldHoarders designed were things of long ago. People no longer killed each other in order to survive on the planet.

Instead, they devoted time toward trying to keep the planet from dying and to start a re-birth a thousand years ahead in the future, the future I now called my home. The clean Earth of the Vision Fold ruled the Tee-Pod Community, and I was the first to arrive in this renewed world. So why was I dreaming of things I studied in history? There was no threat now. I was the only one here.

I thought again about the male in my dream being force fed the poison and felt Tarron's trainings sting my heart. I would not be able to attempt to poison the bear again after having this dream. Deliberately poisoning a living thing would harden my heart and I would feel its pain. As much as I disliked the creature, I would not try it again. I scanned the room. Carmella was still missing.

Steam rose from the pot. The fire was almost hot enough. I removed the last few dried leaves from a basket, crumbled them in my hand and dropped them into one of my new clay cups. I would enjoy tea so much this morning in an uncracked cup. I peered out the window as Carmella skittered in from outside.

"Good morn," I said.

She ignored me and ran onto her rock, slid behind, then came back to the front again. She repeated her dance several times before disappearing. She was playful this morn. What had she eaten?

I poured the steaming water over the tea leaves and left the cup on the counter to sit. I would check while it cooled.

Stepping outside, I inspected the outer ledge of the window and supporting wall for evidence. The branches I'd set down last night lay in tact at the base of the window wall. There were no new claw marks.

Well, the bear hadn't come last night. Good.

Sounds like I'd never heard before startled me from behind. For the first time in a long time I stood frozen. Fear gripped my insides as I thought of the worst. The bear was right behind me!

In that split second, I felt his enormity, heard his walk, but my body stood stiff as a tree trunk, with him just steps away! His mass weight poured a huge shadow on the ground in front of me. It crept in size, growing to cover mine as he approached. I couldn't breathe, couldn't move. Then, in one swift motion I jumped a few feet forward and spun around instinctively to see him. I was terrified.

"Aaaaah!" I screamed looking into the beasts huge nostrils.

But it just viewed the ground, lowered its huge head and ate the herbs that sprung from pieces I'd thrown out the window. I sped around the enormity and the smaller one behind it, into the hillhouse and leapt onto the bedding, covering my head with the blanket, as if it would keep me safe with the door wide open. My heart raced in my head and my body shook itself.

As I waited for Carmella to comfort me I remembered the name of this creature and had to laugh at myself. It wasn't the bear at all, but a spotted animal that could supply meat and drink to us. It was a vegetarian, a Bovidae, a Taurus female. That was the true name, the scientific name, but the ancients called them cows.

Having regained my composure, I

stepped to the window and heard the sticks outside crack at the base of the wall. The littler one wandered to the edge of the hillhouse garden and then returned to the female who was pulling up the grasses, roots and all. She chewed them with her fat green-stained lips. Both were horribly ugly creatures with boxy shoulders, but the little one seemed innocent to me, helpless like an infant back at Tee-Pod. It raised its head to the large one and made the sound again.

"Moo," it said.

I decided I liked them and hoped they would come again after today. From now on I would throw all the herbs out the window to entice them, none out the door.

~ ~ ~

The sun hung high, so without rain in the sky I brought Carmella to the hill with me to wait. Please send him today Tarron, a male, for physical strength. It had been a time since I pondered who they would send. Given a choice, I preferred it be Aldo. He never turned away from my look. He was quiet and agreeable and would likely follow my lead.

I suspected he wouldn't be the one sent, though. He was smaller than many of the others. It would be just as well if they didn't send him. Aldo was not a great strength in any manner and I wanted a male with great strength. Would it be Dallas? CarMickael? Jose? They were the strongest males in the academy, all much larger than I. Surely Tarron would choose one of them.

None of their minds or personalities appealed much to me, but perhaps they had grown changed as I had these past three years. It would be nice when he got here. I'd have much needed help. He could hunt, help make tools, cut real firewood and build an extra room into the house for smoking the meat. That way I wouldn't have to worry about the bear breaking the smoke house wall and stealing my hunt and all that work away again. A muscular male would prove so useful and I welcomed the thought of him. Companionship was companionship at this point, though. Whoever arrived would be welcomed, whether he appealed to me or not.

As I waited on the hill, I braided the

stems of flowers to dry, and finished stitching a few rabbit pelts together.

I thought again of making paint. I remembered the recipes. It would be nice to duplicate the greens and blues in the clean world onto birch bark, or such. I could set them upon the walls of the hillhouse like the ones I'd seen on the videos from the ancient's box computers.

Three birds flew overhead and settled onto the tops of trees in the distance. What power, the ability to fly. This was indeed a beautiful place. I loved the clean world. Clouds passed by as usual, but today there were fluffy ones that layered themselves in the sky, one beneath the other, in whimsical patterns of musical instruments. I remembered the music from Tee-Pod celebrations and hummed along. For a brief moment, I allowed myself the rare pleasure of missing home.

It was getting late. No one came. No one ever came. One-hundred-eighty-eight Tuesdays, still no one came. I breathed in the fresh air and closed my eyes, enjoying the fragrances of the grasses and herbs.

A distant sound caught my attention.

The wind picked up. It was best to get back to the hillhouse when strong winds came. Carmella in hand, I started down the hill.

Tolomay's World and The Pool of Light

ChapTer Eight

The sky screamed a deafening pitch. I turned in time to see the glowing blue water pour, as a spring from a rock, in mid-air before me. Then the sound of the toners chorus burst through the slit.

Before I could think it, a body shot toward me at great speed. It forced the breath from my lungs and me to the ground, then landed hard upon me. Just as fast, a second bolted through and rolled a somersault to the grasses beside us. The Pool of Light flashed brightly before disappearing with a loud and thunderous *clap*.

I took back my breath, pulled myself out from underneath the weight, and disbelieving what I was seeing, stared at the male in front of me. His skin glowed bright red. He seemed as though he was dying.

The female ran to the male who lay

lifeless. She shook his shoulders violently.

"Kenter!"

His eyes opened, he viewed me, and proceeded to lose his food upon the ground before us. There wasn't much in his stomach. It took me a moment to gather my thoughts.

His body shook with fervor as he attempted to speak.

"Leth," he said with a wrenched face as he reached to the female and grasped her arm.

He caught sight of me before closing his eyes again. His face and hands were so red. He was hot as I pressed my ear to his chest. He was breathing.

The female's eyes widened. She viewed me as if I had nine heads, clearly thought I was evil itself with my look, but never mind that. I had to think it! I recognized none of their words. *Leth? Kenter?* Which dialect was that? Which? I shouted to her frantically while she knelt crying over him.

"Zabra Zevo!"

"Deka tapo de mi esillot alyaho!"

"inn abrolen!"

"Jei ta!"

"Recogeril!"

What would they speak? Which one?

Finally, I thought it.

"Pick him up!" I barked in Merican.

She hesitated only for a second before lifting his shoulders. With me at his ankles, we raised him off the ground. Before we took a step, I set his feet back to the grasses to remove Carmella from the stack of braided flower stems where she'd landed. I placed her on my shoulder and took up the male's legs again. We headed slowly downward toward the hillhouse.

He was heavy and slipped from our fingertips so we stopped several times on the way. Wrapping the dark fabric from his garb around our hands for a more secure hold, we repositioned our grip on him at his shoulders and knees, until the next adjustment. We did this several times. Each time, I checked for breathing. He was alive.

Soon enough, we arrived at the hillhouse. He groaned as he was lowered upon my blanket. The female eyed the room cautiously while I retrieved skins and a bowl of medicinal vinegar from the kitchen. When I returned, she was sitting beside him shaking and weeping. I felt the sting of my first experience here, but there wasn't time for wet cheeks. I had to wake him. The vinegar of onion, garlic and mint soaked quickly into the rabbit skin which sank to the bottom of the bowl. It dripped heavily as I drew it back out and handed it to her.

"Rub this on him. All over."

"Where is the med lab?" she asked, desperation pouring from her voice.

"I am trained in curation," I answered.

I set the bowl between us as she stared at me with great apprehension. There was no time for hesitation, but I remained silent as she smelled the cloth. She was leery of me, though I was correct... and after all, what choice could she have? I watched her slide the soaked suede across the top of his hand.

"Begin at his face," I corrected.

The male awoke, gasping and coughing, as soon as the stinking cloth dampened his nose.

"Hey," she said to him as he reached for her.

He was weak just now, no matter his obvious strength. She held his palm in one of hers and dabbed the vinegar on his cheek with the other.

"You made it," she said.

"I was born for this," he replied.

I sat amazed, grateful that Tarron had finally sent someone and not one... but two.

Tolomay's World and The Pool of Light

Chapter Nine

Although he fell right back to sleep, Lethia held Kenter's palm for the longest while. She continued to rub his skin with the vinegar mixture as the younger female instructed. Lethia watched her working in the kitchen, mixing a batch of wound sap for Kenter's face, hands, and feet. The Pool of Light burned him badly during passage. Though no expert, Lethia knew if medicine wasn't applied soon, his skin would blister fiercely, and then shed. She did not trust this one, but she seemed to know curation well enough. Was anyone else here? What of the pod's Originals?

The female returned to the twins, lizard on shoulder, bowl in hand, and settled herself on the stool near the bedding and the two new arrivals.

"Thank you," said Lethia.

Introductions had not been made.

"I'm Lethia," she said. "This is Kenter, my brother."

"I'm Tolomay," the female replied.

It was the first time Tolomay had spoken her name aloud in three years and it sounded strange to hear it. She felt uncomfortable and remained otherwise quiet, as if she couldn't decide what to say.

Lethia thought the circumstance quite *off*. Now that they had arrived, why had the strange female not fetched others?

"We thought it perhaps the Originals had not made it through," said Lethia. "...the equipment... well, the machine failed during transport. Where are they...the elders from the pods? Are they... alive?"

Horrified at the question, Tolomay stared as Lethia's eyes scanned the quaint room, looking for a sign of them. The twin was dark haired with almost black eyes. Silence gnawed at the walls.

"Each have single pods here?" Lethia asked another question before Tolomay answered the first.

Tolomay was surprisingly uncomfortable with this stranger asking questions. She had waited three years for companionship. What was wrong with her? Why couldn't she speak?

Kenter opened his eyes. He faced his sister, but his pain kept him motionless. The females hadn't noticed. Tolomay swallowed hard before answering.

"I was the first through," she said.

Though he could not see her, hearing another articulate those words cut at his heart. He did not turn his head. *He* was meant to be the first. He felt it deep in his core, in every cell of his being. At present, because he felt so incredibly weak, the fact he was not first bothered him even more. The others had survived the passage. He was utterly and cruelly disappointed.

"What do you mean?" asked Lethia. "Where are the Originals from the pods?"

Tolomay stood trembling, her face solemn. She wanted to run from the room and out the door, through the grasses and away from her shame of having survived when the rest of her team had not. What would these two think of her? She swallowed again, then answered in almost a whisper.

"None behind me survived the swim," she said.

Kenter's heart sank as he instantly understood what she meant, what she was saying. Not only was she one of the Originals, she was the only survivor. What she must have gone through. He felt great remorse for his most recent thoughts, but his sister wasn't picking things up as quickly. When Kenter turned to view the female, he stared in disbelief.

Lethia's face contorted to a perplexed expression.

"But, you're…" she began, and then stopped herself. She couldn't say what she was thinking. "so young," she said instead.

"I'm sixteen," replied Tolomay.

"I do not understand. The Originals were sent thirty years ago," said Lethia. "Where did *you* come from and how did you get here?"

"The passage travels to the same light point." Kenter's interruption startled them both. "Remember your time math, Leth."

Tolomay shot a quick look to him and caught his glance. He did not flinch at her look, and instead fixed his eyes upon hers.

"You've been here…three years?" he

asked.

She stared without answering.

"By yourself?" he asked.

Tolomay nodded and her gaze fell to the floor.

The sister finally understood. But how could it be? And the female looked so desperately young.

"So, *you* are from one of the pods?" asked Lethia, still disbelieving.

"From Tee-Pod," answered Tolomay.

"But how can you..." Lethia changed her words again. "That would mean when they sent you, you were the age of ..."

Tolomay and Kenter answered before she could finish.

"Thirteen," they said together.

Lethia stared at the lizard resting on Tolomay's shoulder, then at the scant items around the room.

"Then, all of this..."

"I did it," answered Tolomay.

As odd as it was, it made sense to Lethia. At first glance the structure appeared sound, but the construction was incredibly amateurish. The simplest of steps had been skipped. Certainly the child must have been weak at just thirteen turns, so no wonder the smallness of the too numerous and rough planks, especially here, without proper tools.

Lethia's eyes found the ceiling beams. Still, she decided, this was a solid enough roof in a clean world, and the very first. They would make due for the time being. After all, this child had survived in this hillhouse for three years on her own. In all certainty they could learn a thing or two from her.

Kenter's thoughts were elsewhere. Mouth open, he looked intently at this female, this Original. As strange as her appearance was, he was fascinated by it. She had the look of the ancient Coin Makers, the GoldHoarders he'd studied in history training, but he was not afraid of her. On the contrary, he was in awe.

He closed his mouth, but could not stop his eyes from staring. He had never seen golden hair or blue eyes on anyone living.

ChapTer Ten

I was suddenly anxious. *'Three years,'* Kenter had said. *'By yourself.'* I somehow felt diminished in their eyes, not the confident one who'd barked orders at Lethia to pick him up when he came through injured.

At the time, I was concerned for the male's life, so of course, I'd issued orders. With nothing urgent needed, my tongue fell silent. I scratched Carmella's neck. This male was not one I knew and neither was she. He was muscular though, so his strength would do. How had Tarron trained new candidates in only three years? Where in the pods had they lived that I had not met them before? And what was time math? I'd never heard of it.

I wished he would stop staring. Was the cause of it pity? Pity did nothing for my heart and, if anything, made me feel weak and vulnerable. It was the only thing that could bring my tears, and this was not the time for them. What of the community rules of courtesy? Did he stare at all in this manner?

I worried that he knew of me and my mother, but then it dawned on me that perhaps he thought it I was simply a frail young thing. No. In all certainty, I'd been correct at first. Of course my look is why he stared. Why wouldn't he? He must think my hair hideous. It infuriated and shamed me terribly. But I could not think it now; so all the same, and just as quickly, I remembered how long I awaited this company before me. As I pushed away my suspicion and guilt, I pulled a new thought to me and warmth once again filled my heart.

I was elated Tarron had sent a male for physical strength and the extra hands of a female. No matter that he was not one I expected. More would come soon enough and we could start the first settlement much easier with three of us. Not as easily as if the others who travelled with me had lived, but three sets of hands would be much better than one.

I now had a community of my own. Perhaps we wouldn't have to wait as long for Tarron to send others. I wondered if Vision Fold's equipment would hold enough power this time to send candidates more regularly. I did not want to wait another year or two, or maybe three, for more.

I felt his eyes follow me to the kitchen even as I turned to sit on the stump. As soon as I met his gaze, his look fell away and he turned toward the female. She continued applying wound sap to his shaking hands. She was beautiful, with long flowing hair. Her almost black eyes stopped my thoughts.

"Well," she said tenderly. "You made it through fairly unscathed. We're here."

He acknowledged her words with a smile and then turned back to view me again. What was wrong with his manners that he did not turn away? He would not stare so long for my mere look... or had I hung my shame so loudly upon my face? Lethia finished a second coat on his cheeks, and dropped the animal skin into the nearly empty bowl.

The male's straight black hair lay as a

backdrop to the wound sap that covered his face and stuck to his eyebrows. He looked like a pasty yellow owl with mad eyes. He would look this way for a few days, even after a good wash up at the stream. Wound sap worked better than anything for burns, cuts and lesions, but always stained the skin the yellow color of the flower it was harvested from. The paste would dry soon though, and I was not yet done. He would need aloe and bandages applied if I were to do the job correctly. I had to fetch the aloe.

"I, uh, I must go out," I said and turned out the door. I felt the both of them watch me leave. Perhaps I *had* forgotten my social skills. Should I have said something more?

I harvested three large aloe leaves from the sandy berm. As I walked back, two dark figures loomed at the edge of the grasses. It was the Bovidae! They had returned! I hurried to the hillhouse. This was the first time in three years there was someone to share my excitement with. I was so ecstatic I nearly fell through the doorway before closing the door and leaping the few steps to the kitchen.

"Come to the window!" I urged, rushing to the counter. "Come see the Bovidae!"

The two glanced at one another. They both seemed taken aback at my boldness. Perhaps my demeanor *had* needed improving, but a Bovidae! How could they not be beside themselves with anticipation? Lethia stood, but only Kenter spoke.

"Window?" he asked.

What? I thought it for a moment. Was my Merican translation accurate? Window...I was right.

"To see out," Lethia explained to him.

To my amazement, I realized he did not know what a window was. He didn't know what a window was? How could he not? I leaned forward, rubbed the sill and put my hands through the opening.

"Window," I said.

He nodded. Lethia stepped beside me. Kenter, not yet strong enough, stayed on the bedding, but managed himself to a sitting position.

"What it is, Leth?" he asked.

"The most amazing thing," she answered in almost a whisper. "It is as the ancient's photos. There is a large creature on this Earth. It walks like a dog, but it is bigger than a dog, bigger than us."

"Bigger than us?" he asked in disbelief.

Lethia did not answer. We both watched as the great one ate grasses and the littler one poked at the larger one's belly with its nose.

"Oh!" she continued. "There are two! One is an infant."

Hearing that, Kenter tried to rise. He seemed determined not to miss this glorious sight. When he almost fell, Lethia and I each supported one of his arms from underneath, at his chest, and escorted him to the window. He felt very hot and truly heavy, but I did not care. I watched the smiles of joy that painted their faces.

Kenter gasped as he saw the world.

"Green," he said in amazement.

I had forgotten he had not paid mind to the landscape when he came through. He likely noticed nothing but his pain. Lethia pointed to the creatures.

"It's all so green," he repeated.

His body shook.

"Look, Kenter!" said Lethia, her

finger aimed at the beasts, then she turned to me as if to ask their name.

"Bovidae," I said, "It's their family name."

My heart skipped a beat as the male viewed them then smiled at me with great warmth. His mad yellow owl mask cracked at the corners of this mouth. When the paste split where his lips turned up and at the centers of his beaming cheeks, my joy all but forced a laugh from me. I was so happy. I had a community and there were three of us. We could share the joy together.

"Bovidae," he repeated before his eyes rolled closed.

He fell back into sleep with us holding him. Lethia and I carried his shaking body to the bedding and rested his head on the rabbit fur. I gathered the aloe from the counter while Lethia puffed the bedding beneath him to raise his feet. He was still in a level of shock, but I did not worry. It was likely as severe sun poisoning would be. There was little more I could do but feed the wounds aloe, so I reassured myself he would recover fully.

After scraping the gel from the leaves, I made the aloe paste and spread it carefully onto his yellow mask and around his hands, wrists, ankles, and feet. I sat and watched him sleep. He would heal. The combination would keep moisture in and infection out. I covered it loosely in skins and secured them in place. It would dry slower this way, and none of its curing properties would be left to the air. Then I started work on the Aspir for his pain. Fresh burns are most painful. Kenter would be in for a restless sleep tonight.

Chapter Eleven

Kenter's skin burned and his knees felt weak. He smelled something good as he stepped clumsily out the door. His muscles had a mind all their own when his feet landed on Earth's soft, thick carpet.

He turned his attention to the clean world. He opened his heart to it the moment he'd seen the greens in the grasses and the magestical Bovidae creatures, making the decision right then that he would never tire of nature.

For no matter how detailed the research or the professor's descriptions had been during training, or how the ancient's photos appealed to him; none had done this world justice. He could never, in his wildest dreams, have imagined a place as perfect. Being here sent the heat he had dreamed of into his heart.

After spending so much time laid beneath the bedding, it was good to stretch out his limbs, though every ounce of him hurt. The burns would take a while to heal. Thoughts of Mize Maxy's lectures on the use of wound sap poured though his mind. The old male did know a bit about medicinal herbology and curation after all.

Lethia and the female were nowhere in view. He couldn't quite remember what his sister said when she woke him briefly some time ago, but it surprised him to find himself alone in the dirt pod when he opened his eyes. He had never been alone in such a large space. It was uncomfortable, but at the same time, freeing. He breathed in the air. The fragrance was unbelievable.

The grasses tickled his toes in the breeze as he sat waiting for his sister and the female to return. Then dizziness crept back to him. He lay down upon the ground, but re-thought it. He did not want the female to find him asleep on the grasses. Though he wasn't sure why, it seemed best to go inside.

A strange aroma lingered in the room. He'd smelled it when he first awoke, but after being outside it seemed a stronger enticement. It was one of edibles, but not ones familiar to his nostrils, not of the foods he was accustomed to.

He found a wooden plate heaping with the largest pieces of beast he had ever seen. Each one was an extremely thick light colored string. They were almost clear in places and were enormous, a third the length of his thumb. Beside it rested another plate full of mysterious long fruits.

Instantly, his stomach reminded him he hadn't eaten breakfast. He was starving. Sitting on a wooden stump, he wolfed down the huge chunks of beast, eating faster than he'd remembered doing in his lifetime. Some pieces were tender and nearly melted in his mouth, some parts chewy. The taste was strange, but perfect.

The soft green fruit wasn't as good. The outer coating was pleasant enough, but once his teeth crunched past the firm outsides, the inside was gooey; but it was sweet, so none the less, he ate it relentlessly and was satisfied. Even the food in this place tasted purer than back home. A clay bowl lay beside the plate. It held a liquid. He first smelled it and then pursed his lips, brought up the bowl, and tasted the water. It was fresh and magic. No chemical flavors lingered within. He relished its purity, and this moment in time. Would everything in this world be so delicious?

His stomach now full, Kenter viewed the empty plates before him. He wondered if Lethia had left these for him, or if the female had. She must have been so glad they'd arrived she'd thought of him straight away. He was glad for it. He was the first male after all, and always would be.

Taking in his surroundings, he was amazed the young one had accomplished the task of staying alive all this time. How could one lone female do so much without a strong male around, and without so much as a second set of hands? He had never been alone in his whole existence. It was hard to imagine it.

The sound of his sister, giggling, prefaced the females' return. The sixteen year old walked in with a serious but pleasant enough expression.

"I call it the hillhouse...," she said turning back to Lethia who followed her in. "...because this big mound of dirt with grasses is called a hill."

As she hung the water bag near the entryway, Tolomay wondered if her pronunciation was correct. She decided she would speak only Merican to Kenter and Lethia, but would still practice her other languages to Carmella as usual, so she wouldn't lose her spoken tongue.

Tolomay was taken aback at seeing Kenter at the table. She stopped her feet before turning around to close the door behind Lethia. Would he stare at her look again? It unnerved her.

"I'm glad to see you're awake!" said Lethia, stepping to him with a careful hug.

Eyes sparkling with joy, she dropped the basket of flowers to the grass matt and handed him a daisy.

"There are thousands of these, all different colors. And Kenter, you would not believe it how a real stream looks and sounds! There are flying beasts named butterflies. They are as purity itself," she said, then viewed the bandages wrapped to his face.

They covered all of his skin and left holes only for his eyes, nose, and mouth.

"I'm good now," he replied. "I ate."

Tolomay's expression changed as her eyes fled to the empty plates and opened wide. Kenter noticed. Perhaps the dinner had been for all three of them, not just for him.

"Did I eat everyone's?" he started. "I thought it the plates were set out for me."

Lethia cut in.

"He's accustomed to the elite line in the eating room. We get whatever we want there," she said in his defense.

Tolomay was frustrated. She saved for over a week, and had boiled them just today. She did not know how to say what she was thinking. This was not the eating room back home. Had this male no training whatsoever on NOT eating items in the clean world unless he knew what they were, or if they were poisonous?

"No. That was not dinner," was all she could reply.

She rubbed her fingers down the side of her face, until they found her chin. She could not believe it... all that work and saving.

"Well, it was a filling snack," said Kenter, a bit relieved.

Now, he was contemplating how

wondrous the dinners would be.

"It's best not to eat things in the clean world if you do not know what they are," scolded Tolomay.

She stepped forward to pick up one of the empty plates.

"Wasn't it beast and fruit?" he asked.

She stood silent. Was this male an infant? Had he not studied? She could not believe Tarron would send such an untrained candidate into the clean world.

"No," she replied. "This plate held the aloe leaves that will heal your skin, and this," she said, picking up the other, "was stacked with meat fat for making oil. Oil has many uses in this world, cooking, light, and much more. It is precious and takes work to make. Now I am low of it."

Carmella skittered down her arm, landed beside the clay bowl, and began lapping up what little water droplets remained at its bottom.

"And that's Carmella's water bowl," she finished.

The room remained still as Tolomay brought the water bag down from its perch and refilled Carmella's bowl. She was surprised at how arrogant her words sounded, even to her. She swallowed hard, listening as the lizard lapped up the water. Had it been such a long three years that she'd forgotten what it was like to know little of one's surroundings?

"But, yes, the fat *is* from beasts, and the aloe is edible, too. You are safe," she continued, as she set the plates on the counter and reached up toward a shelf. "None are poisonous, though I do not think it that your stomach will forgive you later."

She softened her statement by returning to Kenter with a small clay cup full of raspberries.

"Here," she said, setting it into his bandaged hands. "These are *real* food, and some of the best. And trust it that you will greatly enjoy a genuine dinner in this world tonight," she finished.

The feeling of foolishness left Kenter's heart the moment his tongue tasted the sweet juicy fruit. His eyes grew large. Lethia's fingers raced her brother's into the cup for the next bite and the twins laughed at the play.

ChapTer Twelve

The site of the male's bandaged face when I awoke the next morning startled me. I was surprised to see the two there. Dreams can wipe clean the memories of new things and I had been alone so many days I forgot in one sleep they'd arrived. I stared at the new members of my community as they lay slumbering. The male turned. His burns were hot. Even at this distance, he emanated heat. His moving almost roused him, and no wonder at the pain his skin must carry, but then he closed his half-opened eyes and drifted back away.

Where was Carmella? She lay tucked beneath my knee. I reached for her and pulled her to my chest, then resettled myself on the still bumpy new matt. The floor was not soft as my bedding was. No matter. The injured male needed it more than I.

Excited they were here, I thought it best to start breakfast, but the sleep had not left my mind enough to move further. As I lay listening to my breathing, Carmella slipped deliberately from my hand, ran to the bedding where Kenter lay, and pushed her way beneath it.

I should get up.

I stretched my limbs toward opposite sides of the room to wake my muscles and wondered if the bear came last night. Against the judgment of my shoulders, I sat.

It was strange having two others in the clean world with me, here in the hillhouse. I somehow felt like a host to them. Growing up in a community pod was different. None were hosts there. Community members had specific tasks scheduled into routines, in an effort that all things got done for each.

I'd once read an article ad for dishes, about ancients having been hosts. On the paper was drawn a female in a long dress. She was smiling and offering teacups and food arranged on a large round tray to citizens sitting, one beside the next, on an odd wide chair. None of us at the academy practiced the ancient tradition. I had no tray, but there were my cups and plates as we used last eve.

This was peculiar, but since there had been no actual training available on this subject, the brother and sister would know it no different. I would calculate for myself the right way to work it.

Like last night's dinner, today's breakfast should be the most splendid, since it would always be their first. The best would be eggs, if I could find them, crabapple buds, and perhaps sprinkled with wheat beads and crushed bits of nuts. Yes. I would have to boil the crabapple buds as they were not nearly mature, but I could cook away some of their bitterness and then they would do nicely. I left the siblings to their dreams and stepped into the grasses that welcomed my feet each morning. My heart leapt. I had *company*. That made it the most wondrous morning since I'd arrived and it felt delicious to my heart.

While I ate breakfast, I watched Lethia scoop food into Kenter's mouth as if he were a one year old infant. I found it odd. He could, after all, surely move his hands. He had last night. After a few feeble attempts at struggling to hold the spoon with his bandaged hands, she took over without a word from him. But, perhaps it was not strange, for I had no brother who needed healing so I did not know.

Still, he ate his entire plateful and then drank two full cups of water. The drinking, he managed on his own. It was good he liked the breakfast. He needed nourishment. Once she stood to put the plates in the kitchen, I took my turn at his side checking the bandages. I was after all, the medical herbologist and had been trained extensively in curation. It was my expertise, which came in handy for knowing what to eat as well. My training in these areas had been one of the things that saved my life since, Marva, the food guide, perished with the rest of my team upon entry. I shuttered at the thought.

~ ~ ~

The bandages remained moist enough to easily pull from Kenter's cheek, but the pain would not allow it. At the surface, the burns appeared no worse than a severe sunburn, but the physics by which he was burned affected the integrity of even the lowest level of skin, quite possibly the tissue beneath.

Time energy was much more powerful than the heat of the sun. It changed molecular configuration to some degree during passage and reconfigured it at the end. I'd leave these bandages alone for now and recheck them later today. He didn't need to be in more pain at present. The coating of aloe seemed intact, so I saw no reason for concern. The wounds might take an extra week or two longer than I'd originally thought, but they would heal, none the less.

His sister appeared more concerned than I.

"How does it feel?" she asked.

Kenter looked up at me.

"It's fine, Leth," he replied.

"Are you full?" I asked him.

He viewed his sister. Apparently he was not, but would not say so.

"I'll prepare something more." I said. "You need your strength."

"Thanks," he answered.

While more crabapple buds boiled, Lethia sat beside her brother. I brought him a handful of shelled nuts, and placed them directly into his bandaged hand. He chewed them, moaning in ecstasy the whole while.

I remembered the feeling of magic touching my palate each time I ate when first arriving in the clean world. The food in this place was glorious. I handed Lethia a few and ate some as well. We each smiled at our mouthful of delight.

"The trees offer these freely to the ground when they are done with them," I said. "They are the easiest protein foods to find. But they come only in seasons, so I save now. Squirrels like to steal the work to gather as their own. So, we must keep the bag tied."

Later in the day, while Kenter slept, I took Lethia to my garden. The area was fenced with large branches I collected in the woods. It took nearly two weeks to pound them into the ground with a rock my first season here; each butted up to the next, until the border of sticks stood together as tightly as fingers, side by side.

I did it in order to surround the area where I selected to plant. It was the only way I knew to keep the rabbits out. I laid herbs in rows like those in the lab's supply garden. Medicinal herbs were in the front, except for the aloe and wound sap. Those two would not grow here.

They were finicky about their soil and preferred to be left unmanaged. In the middle section grew the parsley, chives, sage, oregano and basil. Thyme, dill and tarragon stood in the back along with others. I broke off a piece of basil and gave it to Lethia.

"Chew it," I advised.

She sniffed at it, then ate it slowly, as if her tongue pondered its new discovery. Her eyes brightened. Then I told her the names of them all and handed her a handful, a little of each.

Her face beamed as she smelled them, breathing in each as if it were her last sacred breath of air.

"Taste them, too," I urged. "They are to eat and to season with. They share their flavor and nutrition with the other foods in the pot."

"I trained in cooking," she said. "But our flavors came from bits. We never had these."

"Only the science division gets the use of them when they're fresh," I responded. "Tarron used to treat me. I have many mints, too, on the other side of the hillhouse."

Lethia's eyes lit.

"They spread. Thyme and mint can

keep mosquitos away, too."

I could see it in her eyes she did not know of the pests.

"Mosquito's are tiny, nearly invisible, but vicious insects, bugs. They like to bite and leave their marks as red spots all upon my skin and can make us very ill if we do not use the plants. These help keep us tasting sour, so they do not come. Well, not as much. Lemongrass and lavender work toward that as well. I will show you how to mix them."

Lethia nodded as I walked to the corner and pointed to another group of plants.

"These will show red fruits later. Tomatoes. The ancients thought them poisonous for many eons, but they are nutritious and sweet and they pop when you bite them. They're fun to eat. Tiny seeds hide inside, but the fruits grow this large," I said, and balled my fist to show her.

Her eyes widened. I pointed to other green leaves.

"There are edibles beneath these. They are good. Potatoes, but not big enough yet. They like the cold and wet. There too, roots hidden beneath," I said, pointing to another group a short distance away with leaves that look like grasses.

I broke one piece off and handed it to her. When she smelled it, her nose crinkled up and I laughed. She did not care for its strength of odor.

"Onions," I smiled. "They are sweet when you cook them. They sweeten other foods in the pot and can help to heal most illnesses. You uncover them with this," I said, grabbing up the small wooden shovel that lay against the fence. "You dig them up. Oh... and these."

I stepped to a group of ruffled leaves huddled together nearest the gate. I set the edge of the spade to the earth beside the largest plant and pushed down. The ground rebelled.

"It is dry. It's not always," I explained, and then scraped the blade around the plant.

Using the looser dirt as a guide, I stuck the blade in again and stepped on it hard, but not too hard. I did not want to break another shovel; they took days to make properly. This time the earth crumbled around its edge. I pulled at the green leaves and wiggled the shovel back and forth until the root escaped from its hiding place, then re-covered the hole with the loose dirt and set the shovel back against the fence. I handed the orange root to Lethia.

"It's a carrot," I said. "Try it. It's good."

Her eyes spoke delight at its taste.

"I've heard of carrots," she said.

"You'll love the ginger. It's very sweet and strong. Oh, and the rosemary. It's on the other side of the hillhouse. I'll show you now, a huge bush," I said. "I love it with squirrel."

I carefully closed the gate behind us as we left the garden to itself.

"If the gate is not closed tightly, the rabbits will eat all of my herbs... our herbs," I corrected myself. "Then we will have to forage. Trust me in it; you do *not* want to forage except for pleasure and exploration to find new ones, but not out of necessity. Nutrition is the thing, and to keep some herbs nearby for flavor is best. The bear got to them his first year and it was a hard season for me, but he has no interest in them now." I said.

"I studied of rabbits," Lethia said.

"The blankets here, the ones I make, are of rabbit and squirrel fur," I answered. "Rabbit is softest."

"I know of beavers, too, she replied. "They build their own homes, and in water at that. I don't remember my beasts well enough, though," she said. "Which one is a bear?"

Once again, I thought of Tarron. He trained differently than the community's new instructor, Mize Maxy, did. Had Tarron trained Lethia and Kenter, they would have more knowledge regarding creatures and food in this world. I could not believe my father would allow the Vision Fold to send such ill prepared candidates to swim. Apparently things changed drastically in the years since I'd left, and not for the better. Lethia stopped walking. She had asked about the bear.

"The bear...," I said with a loud breath. "A bear is a mammal. They give live births and the one here has brown fur. They walk on four legs, but can walk on two if they choose. Not normally though, normally all four. Their body structure is very massive. They like to be pesky and ruin things that take weeks to make. They eat meat, so don't approach him for any reason, but they also eat fruits and herbs. He has big teeth and hands... paws. The bear who comes to this area likes smoked meats and fur blankets and he scratches his claw marks on the hillhouse," I blurted out.

Lethia stood as if in awe of my brilliance, or so I thought, before she laughed unexpectedly. I had spoken the string of words rapidly and nearly without a breath between thoughts. I had to laugh back. I'd amused her tremendously and it really was funny.

"You don't like this bear creature, do you?" she asked, still laughing.

"No. I do not. He's horrid," I said, depositing a leaf from the carrot top onto my tongue, "And he's not afraid."

Chapter Thirteen

Carmella skittered across the room and tucked herself behind her rock. The three sat on the bedding, Tolomay stitching in the last square of rabbit fur. She cut the loose strapping with her cutting stones and handed the finished blanket to Lethia.

"I'm glad I had enough pelts," she said, "Now we each have one."

"Thank you," Lethia remarked with a smile.

She squeezed her fingers deep into the soft piece of heaven, then rubbed its fur against the side of her cheek. Tolomay turned to Kenter.

"To answer your question, I expected only a male. That's what we were told. But we were five in my group. So why did Tarron send only two of you?" Tolomay asked him.

"Tarron?" Kenter replied, finishing the last of his salad.

He set the bowl onto the dirt floor, and then scratched briefly at the bandages around his eyeholes.

"Tarron Elms, of the Literary Division. Apparently he mentored her in herbs and such and allowed her tastes of them," said Lethia.

Tolomay crinkled her brow. She never met nor heard of Tarron Elms.

Lethia turned to her brother, to offer him a feel of her blanket. He dug his fingers into the fur, then shook his head with a smile.

"Think it, Leth. He is too young to be there thirty years ago," he reminded her, then grinned at his coming tease. "The brilliant carpentry architect who could never grasp time math."

"Elms?" Tolomay wondered aloud.

Her father was Tarron *Ramey*, head of the Science Division. Tarron was the one who gave birth to '*Vision Fold.*' He was responsible for the Pool of Light project. Without Tarron's device, none of them would be here. No candidate even went through training without his seal of approval first. Everyone knew

Tarron, pillar in the science field. He hand selected each candidate. How could they not know him personally? Perhaps he had moved up to head the senate like he dreamed of. But even at that, the twins would surely know *of* him.

"Tarron heads the science community. How do you not know that?"

Then a thought struck her like a falling branch. It folded her heart inside itself and dread followed the sensation into her stomach. She felt her expression fade. There was but one reason she could fathom that they would not know Tarron.

"You mean Tarron *Ramey*," Kenter said slowly, as a statement more than a question.

"Yes," she replied softly.

Something was wrong. Kenter saw it that she did not want the truth.

"How do you know of him?" he asked. "He selected you to swim?"

"He is my father," she said, forcing the words from her throat.

She watched his lips. There were words she did not want to hear lurking in his mouth.

At Tolomay's last words, the one of

Tarron being her father, Lethia stopped caressing her blanket and turned to watch her brother. Kenter never expected to have the fast approaching conversation with anyone who had a parent, least of all a sixteen year old female who'd lived alone for three years.

Tolomay's look pleaded with him not to answer, as a pool swelled at the base of her crystal blue eyes. In one swift moment, a tear ran down her cheek. She knew. She knew what he was about to tell her; her father had died. He could not help his eyes watering to match her pain.

"I'm sorry," was all he could muster as he dropped his gaze, setting his bandaged palm atop hers. She swiftly reclaimed her hand, and rose to a stand.

"No," she said, refusing his answer.

The twins sat unmoved as she stepped out the door, her cheeks dripping water. They were of no use to comfort her. She did not really know them at all.

Hours later the water stopped coming as she lay curled in anguish beneath a tree in her favorite section of field. She felt the heat from her swollen cheek and the side of her nose sticking them to the grasses.

When she finally sat and pressed her palms to her face, the rippling effect of the blades of grass stayed their place, leaving imprints. Her neck was wet. She rubbed its tickle away and wiped her eyes. She had not cried as long since her first day in the clean world and was utterly exhausted. She needed food and drink, and home. What would they think of the way she had abandoned them there?

Tolomay always knew Tarron would no longer be alive when she arrived in the clean world. It was fact she saw evidence of. This place was, after all, a thousand years in his future. But she always felt him near, that he was on the other side of the time divider, thinking of her as often as she thought of him. She felt so close to him it was as if her father lived here in this time with her.

Discovering he died even before Kenter's and Lethia's swim was a grievous feeling, almost one of betrayal. She'd never experienced so much pain. Being scared and alone in the clean world and knowing Tarron was there loving her and thinking of her every day, and perhaps catching a glimpse of her in a reflection from time to time, was an entirely different feeling than being here in the clean world with others, while knowing Tarron was not alive in his.

Even with them here, she now felt more alone than before. It made no logical sense, but was a matter for her heart, and her feelings regarding it were what they were. She missed her father.

After drawing what strength she could from her world, she returned home to the first hillhouse surprise she'd known. Kenter's bandaged face was asleep on the bedding, but Lethia had fetched stream water as Tolomay'd shown her to do just yesterday. She tried her hand at cooking what was in the house, which smelled strongly of food.

Fresh flower blooms adorn the table, thickly covering its top from end to end, like a brilliant velvet cloth; blankets were neatly tucked atop of the two sitting stumps. It was on that day she truly discovered she no longer had to be by herself in the world, unless she chose to.

"Thank you," she said as Lethia stepped closer. After touching the female's bright red cheeks, the twin brought Tolomay closer with a hug.

Once again tears found their way down her cheeks.

"You are not alone, now," Lethia said, as the sixteen year old sobbed into the shoulder and comfort of a friend.

Tolomay's World and The Pool of Light

ChapTer Fourteen

I dampened it before trying to peel up the bandage further, but still it tore at the skin.

"Bombs!" Kenter shouted, as he jerked his head away.

Blood trickled down his cheek. He wrinkled his brow and sucked air in through his teeth.

"Oooh, it bleeds," I said, reaching back to his face with the cloth.

It soaked the red in quickly as I applied pressure to the skin.

"The head always bleeds," I explained.

Lethia raised her brow to her brother.

"You shouldn't say *bombs*," she scolded, in the calm that often held her voice.

"Bad language follows pain," I said, "No matter."

She was surprised. It was the first

time I had come to Kenter's rescue, but only because I caused the hurting. It was usually Lethia's task to make excuses for him. After a few minutes, I pulled the edge of the bandage just enough to peek at the wound, but his hand raced to mine at the first sign of pain. I was uneasy at his warm fingers. A male had never touched my skin and it took my breath away and quickened my heart; just as swiftly, though, he took the cloth from my hand and applied pressure to his cheek himself.

"I've got this," he said.

I wondered why his skin felt so hot. Were the burns curing correctly?

I stood and took a step back, dropping my gaze to the walls as he stared at me, no longer as concerned by his stares. That was just how he was. I worried on his healing. The sores would require more wound sap and aloe, and to dampen the edges enough to peel away the bandage without tearing the skin. Then I could reapply the sap and paste to the tender blisters. Bacteria can't easily access wounds that are closed. Staying away infection was my only real focus.

As I readied myself to fetch the herbs,

I left Lethia at the foot of the bedding where she always was, doting over her brother.

She sat trying her hand at stitching rabbit skins together. Having broken two of my needles already, she was failing miserably. I'd have to make more. Obviously the tolerance and patience she maintained concerning her brother's dependency on her, she lacked in the stitching of pelts. Had she been the injured one, I doubted she would have remained in bed for six days straight, being catered to night and day like a toddler. I would not have done that.

Before stepping out the door, I stared at her, thinking how this was not as I had dreamed it would be. I was doing much of the work, and now for three of us. Lethia caught my gaze on my way out as if she read my disappointment.

I complained to myself with each step toward the herbs. It was ridiculous. The male had no fever heat, no broken bones, and though his burns would leave numerous scars, they were still somewhat superficial wounds. His skin had not charred nor shed. He would heal fine if I kept infection at bay.

The most that would happen would

be the skin would crack a bit later, at the end of his healing. Other than that, in another week or two he would be healed… if his bones and muscles didn't seize up first, from lack of movement… from laziness.

The twins' dynamics were clear to me. I liked both of them enough, but abhorred the fact that Lethia babied the male. My lips could never speak these thoughts, if I were to keep peace with the only company I'd had in three years. I was in a crossfire of emotions.

The cool air felt good on my face. Fragrances of the field and wild flowers surrounded me. I relished the way it blew about in the air of pinks and oranges and blues. The trees danced to the sunset in a most perfect way. I rubbed at Carmella's neck, just as she liked. I felt her love for me. It was wonderful to be out here, but the singing sky and sweet aroma proved only a temporary distraction to my frustration as I continued my steps away from the hillhouse.

While I did feel sorry for Kenter's injuries, and was worried that the bandages did not easily release his skin, I was growing very tired of the two of them having their private sympathy celebration for him. It was as though he thought he would be king in this world when he arrived. I saw arrogance and did not approve.

Brother and sister, or not, I was an Original and the one who would lead us. No matter what they had trained for, my experience would help us survive in the clean world, and the longer they were around me the more they began to realize the truth of it. Age did not matter here. I knew this world and they did not. Not yet. In many ways it was empowering, but I genuinely hated it. I was tired of always being strong, tired of the burden.

Kenter's healing could not come soon enough for me. Then he could share in the work load. The male was sent here for physical strength, not to be spoiled. Had he come alone, things would be as they should be. Had Lethia not been here, I would have made him move about these past few days without her objections. After all, circulation was good for healing.

Like a lightning strike it hit me, and the instant shamed my heart. I was jealous. Not of Kenter's spoiling, but of having to share him with his sister.

Had my vision for myself been set so firmly in stone? Had my desire to have a physically strong male with me been so engrained in my mind that it affected my ability to see clearly? Perhaps a bit. Still, I saw plainly enough to know that his sister's catering to Kenter could prove a problem for us all. We, each of us, had to have the ability to garner our own individual strength. Had I been as dependent as Kenter, I surely would have perished by now.

I removed my shoes to rub my toes upon the sandy dirt. The wind always blew it into drifts on one side here. It felt calming. As I scrunched my piggy's up and down, I pulled at the fattest of the succulent's offerings, finally ripping the section of aloe in half with my fingernails at its widest part. I loved the scent of fresh aloe goo as it oozed from the bottoms of the pokey leaves. I rubbed the gel against the back of my hand and took in its odor. It smelled so perfect.

It was a struggle to tear the other aloe leaves away from their mother plant, but I needed to bring full leaves. The lower one plucked, the thinner and drier it got. I had to twist and bend the base of the leaves to release them from the parent's protective grip.

The air had been hot these past days, and the ground spoke. It begged for water. Because of that, they were drier than usual so I took extra, just to be certain. Dry leaves always offer a selfish amount of gel. No matter, though. It would be enough, and the eve smelled of rain. They would be happier tomorrow. I bundled them together with strapping, gathered the petals for the wound sap, and set them, one beside the other, in the basket.

The heat of my emotions began to cool with the evening air and my thoughts stood clearer. I would, little by little, keep Lethia from catering to Kenter. I would do so by giving her extra tasks and speak to Kenter privately when he was being weak. He needed to see his weaknesses in order to change them. I would use the gentle methods Tarron had raised me with in his attempts to turn me into a survivor. Why had I not thought this out earlier? After all, I could surely be gentle like my father, couldn't I? Feeling relieved, I headed down the hillside.

I heard him before I saw him, and stopped instantly. The bear emerged from the tree line a hundred yards away.

There he stood.

Frozen in place, I watched as he sniffed at the air. I was down wind, so he could not smell me. He did not look to me or see me. My heart raced, but I was safe. Still, he blocked my path home. That stupid bear. I would have to wait and it was turning to dark.

He paused to rub his back on the tree that stood directly between me and the hillhouse. For long minutes he stood scratching against the sharp bark of the great pine, stopping only when he noticed the light as it shown suddenly through the distant doorway. Oh no! Lethia had opened the door! She stepped out. In the diminishing light of the sunset, her silhouette shown clearly at the doorway before it melted into the dark shadows of the grassy area, as she stepped away from the house.

She'd left the heavy door wide open! I'd have to think it quickly. She would not know how to keep her and Kenter safe, nor that the beast was now making his way toward them.

Chapter Fifteen

Lethia felt dew in the air, as if rain was waiting to take its turn upon the Earth. It was just as Tolomay described. She could not believe it, that air carried weight in itself. She could feel its heaviness before the impending rain. It was glorious. The wind twirled and danced, blowing her hair into her face. She swiped the long strands from her eyes, tucked them behind her ear and shoulder, then scanned the tree line. Tolomay had not yet returned. It was getting darker by the moment.

Because she survived so long alone here and knew this world, Lethia wasn't worried about the female's safety as she was about the dynamics of the household. Something was grating at Tolomay's nerves. It had painted itself clearly on the sixteen-year-old's face when she stepped out the door. She was angry. Lethia wondered why. Perhaps it was because she had to share her space with them. After all it had been hers before they'd arrived and she put every piece of it together with her own two hands. It was hers and hers alone for the entirety of three whole years. It was strange to think of how someone could own a "place," but she could imagine how Tolomay might feel that way.

Lethia had drastically changed her mind about Tolomay. When Kenter and she first arrived in the clean world, Lethia still stood in the mindset of the pod community. The twins were icons there, the first selected to swim since the Pool of Light was shut down. Lethia had been a top student. All she'd seen when she first looked upon Tolomay, after her initial shock of course, was the face of an innocent child.

After all, she looked younger than they did. But since that time, Lethia discerned that the twins were without knowledge of basic things here, and Tolomay was the expert at surviving. Age had no place at deciding who should lead them at present. They all knew it would be the youngest.

She respected and admired Tolomay more than she would have ever guessed. Besides, she and Kenter were, as yet, powerless to use their expertise to contribute to the household in the slightest bit. With Kenter's injured hands healing, he could not help with manual labor. The females were not able to build Lethia's building designs without him. All three sets of hands would be required, and her brother's were strongest.

They'd have to wait and would need to find the Juper before Kenter could use his own training. He needed the tools and metals, but they could not locate them without the Juper. Nothing seemed to be going the way Lethia originally thought it would. She didn't mind though, not really. This place was heaven. There was no hurry. The planet was healthy. In this world, the end of civilization already happened. Since there was no doomsday looming over their shoulders they could breathe easy. Time had no significance in this world. There were no great worries.

From the dark shadows she heard grasses rustling. Footsteps were fast approaching. The sound belonged to Tolomay who rounded the hill and stopped beside her. She set her finger to Lethia's lips to prevent her from talking, while she caught her breath. Something was very wrong. The two were at the side of the house, outside the small kitchen window. Tolomay threw Carmella inside, and then her eyes found Kenter. He was awake, sitting on the stump, eating. He was beside the open door!

The faint sound of panting neared. It came from the other side of the hillhouse, closer to Kenter than to the females. They would not make the distance to get in.

"VABAY! CLOSE THE DOOR!" Tolomay screamed at him wildly. "HURRY!"

His heart leapt from his chest at the look in her eyes. The terror in her voice bade compliance. He'd never moved so quickly as when he jumped from the stump, ran to the heavy door and closed it, sliding the wooden lock log across it as she had shown them to do. He hadn't thought it first; now the females were locked outside. Why?

"What's wrong?" he asked.

His heart first sped and then dropped to his stomach at the loud growl resonating from the other side of the door. The scratching of a heavy claw sent chills deep into his bones, and then the sounds stopped. Suddenly, the door moved, jolting back and forth enough to terrify him as the beast bumped against it several times. Kenter's wide eyes flew to the window.

"STAY INSIDE!" Tolomay screamed and disappeared from view.

Having no entryway into the house, the bear was now interested in only the females. Tolomay already knew what to do.

She grabbed Lethia by her arm, and half dragged her as they ran toward the half-ruined smokehouse. They would have to hide. Night was creeping over them and they could barely see as they stepped. Lethia tripped on the way inside, but as the bear neared, Tolomay whisked her back to her feet and led her by the hand to the far corner wall.

At the bottom, through a broken part of the frame, was a small tunnel with space enough for more than the two of them. She pushed Lethia in first. The tunnel led nowhere, but that did not matter. The bear was too big to reach them or fit inside. They would be safe. His heavy breathing was so loud, each exhale sent waves of terror into Lethia's heart.

He growled in frustration when the sweep of his arm failed to penetrate their cove. Dirt fell to the tunnel entrance, settling in a pile as he pounded at the wall that kept them safe.

When Lethia cried out, Tolomay capped her lips until she took control of her voice. She had learned this lesson before; screams only furried him further. The beast walked about for some time, roaring his anger and knocking into large logs that once belonged to the structure's frame. The whole while, Tolomay rubbed Lethia's shoulder to calm her.

A light inched its way toward them from the distance. It bounced in the darkness, quickly growing larger as it made its way into the small shack. From behind the bear it came. Kenter. His face was aglow with the power that fear had thrust into him. He'd removed the bandages from his face and his skin oozed a bloody red. Another gasp escaped Lethia at the sight of her brother near the bear, but again Tolomay stifled it with her hand long enough to force a determined eye to the twin.

"Do not scream out," she commanded with a serious whisper.

Lethia tamed her lips and nodded.

Kenter looked terrible and fierce and screamed as he swung the enflamed torch back and forth toward the bear. It angered the beast who lunged at him. Each time it approached, Kenter pushed the end of the burning log forward toward the bear. It backed up, then stepped toward Kenter again.

It was a contest of wills, with both wanting to win. Kenter walked slowly backward, leading the beast away from the females and their hiding place. Lethia wanted to follow, to keep her brother in sight. When she gripped Tolomay's arm and tried to pass, Tolomay refused it. This time, at the sounds, her hand clamped tightly as Tolomay ignored the tears streaming down Lethia's cheeks. They were both so afraid.

"You *must* stay silent," she whispered the order. "And when I speak it, move quickly. You must stay with *me*," she said holding a firm grip on Lethia's hand. "You *must*."

Lethia nodded, and Tolomay uncovered her mouth for the last time.

"Now," whispered Tolomay, and the two crawled from the hiding space.

Lethia followed her through the broken side of the smokehouse until they were out of the rubble. Pulling Lethia behind with each step, she watched Kenter and the bear the whole while. The injured male was ten feet away and the twice-his-size bear too near him for her comfort. Tolomay stopped her feet and released her hold of Lethia. Turning her full attention to the bear, she picked up a heavy piece of branch that once helped support the wall, and ran toward the creature and the male. Then, with all her might, she threw the log at the bear's enormous head.

It startled Kenter and he stumbled. Falling to the ground, he dropped the burning stick on his way. Tolomay retrieved it. She screamed as if a creature herself, and step by step pushed the fiery blaze steadily toward the bear she hated; forcing him to back up at a steady pace. The beast found it difficult and his paws came near in an attempt to bat the fire stick. But she persisted, waving the flame back and forth, so close to his face that it almost brushed his fur.

"Aaaaaaaah!" she shouted with all her fury. "GO!"

Finally, bored with the game and the fire he could not conquer, he turned. In an awkward run, he trod off, away from the three, and disappeared into the dark. Tolomay stood watching the night as Kenter righted himself to a stand. Once the growling and panting faded to a short distance, the three ran back to the hillhouse.

She was fuming.

She used her anger to lift the heavy lock log and slid it into place in one false swoop. It took less than a moment and caused a loud booming sound as its end settled into the carved-out nook. When she turned toward Kenter, he feared something possessed her. Her eyes were filled with a crazed fury.

"I said stay INSIDE!" bellowed Tolomay.

He stood shocked.

"Stay inside! Did you not hear me?" she squawked. "Stay inside means stay inside! You quite nearly got us all killed!"

Now he was angry.

"I'll not leave my sister and you out in the night with a beast!" he screamed back. "Are you OFF?"

He removed his arm from around Lethia, and took a step to confront Tolomay, his eyes seething anger.

"You know nothing!" she yelled. "I know him! If I hide in the tunnel, he leaves! You know nothing of it! You *will* follow my words while you're here, Kenter!" she demanded. "We all three need to stay safe, now!"

"Do not shout your anger at *me*!" he screamed.

Tolomay blew out a breath, then swallowed. She was not done, but she would need to calm herself or she would lose even more control over her fear. She was furious, but would choose not to shout further. They were safe. They were... all three of them, safe. She viewed Kenter's bleeding hands and the red running from the raw and open wounds on his face and shook her head.

"Look at you," she said in disgust. "All that work to heal."

Kenter swiped the blood from his

chin and viewed his hand full of red. Bloody streams continued to run from his peeling cheeks, down his face, and onto his chest. He squeezed his palm shut in an attempt to control the aching, which at the truth of her words, had settled itself quite instantly into his body. His adrenalin rush was leaving. For the pain, he was even angrier.

"My healing is my own concern!" he shot back, louder than he realized. "And you do *not* rule me and my sister!" he glared fiercely.

Lethia was clearly terrified. Tolomay stared into her wide open eyes, then set her hand upon the twin's shoulder, but only briefly. She used Lethia's tenderness to force control over herself, over her next words to Kenter. If she did not, the anger that was eager to race from her lips would find its way out again. Lethia was upset enough. Tolomay stared at Kenter and spoke four words aimed venomously at him.

"You *jeopardized* your sister," she said under her breath, but loud enough be heard.

Turning back to Lethia, Tolomay gently swiped away the wet from the female cheeks with the sides of her thumbs, and she then lowered herself down onto her sleeping matt. She pulled her blanket up over her legs as it stuck to her damp and sweaty skin, and then lay back, facing away from the twins. She was furious.

Since he was in rule of himself now, and no longer needed her aid for his healing, the foolish male could stop his own blood tonight. After all, he had screamed it at her... screamed that his healing was his own concern... he'd screamed it. If he knew so much, then he did not need her aid. For certainty... he would not bleed to death from his injuries. In any event, the wounds would clot themselves enough tonight.

Lethia was shocked at what had just played out before her. A female, this younger female, had shouted at her brother. He had come to save them and Tolomay had shouted at him. She could never remember in all her age, anyone shouting at Kenter. Who would think to do it? There were no words for what was happening. Trauma captured Lethia's heart, and she began to tremble of it. This was not real. They had nearly been killed and now fury filled their home.

Kenter picked up a rabbit skin and wiped his chin.

The house was too small that night, the room too quiet, and no one could escape to the solace of the outdoors. The bear was still out there somewhere.

After the argument, Kenter sat to rest on a stump, holding rabbit leather to his wounds, his heart racing with fury. He said nothing further, but chose not to lay upon the bedding, though his body screamed its pain to him for what he had done. He did not want to be near the stubborn female who cared nothing for him, and wanted to listen to the night sounds. He needed to keep protection over them all, to make sure the bear was no longer near the house. He was the male, the protector.

Kenter did not know it, but Tolomay did the same. She lay on the bedding with eyes closed, to hear better. What if she could not keep infection away this time? Would he die of it? Should she aid him now, even against his words of it? She thought it, but did not offer. She was so angry. Not only had she tasked to keep Lethia safe, but she'd had to leave the tunnel in order to keep Kenter safe. Looking asleep, she lay listening for hours, to ensure the bear had in all certainty left, and then her dreams finally took her.

Lethia was too afraid to say anything to either of them after the argument, for fear of being shouted at herself. She wanted to tell the two she was sorry for going outside, she was sorry for forgetting Tolomay's warning and leaving the door open, and that it was all her fault, but she could not bring herself to slice the silence. She worried that perhaps nothing would be
the same after tonight, as she quietly cried herself to sleep.

ChapTer Sixteen

The world flooded back as the morning light touched my eyes to wake me. While I listened to the crackling of embers, shame filled my heart. Not because of last night's anger or for the words I'd spoken. I had been right and knew it. Safety from beasts and nutrition were the most important things in this world and Kenter needed a quick lesson in following directions. But the intensity in which my words exploded into the air during the argument was not acceptable. I'd shouted at him with all my veracity. I'd found my temper and rage all on the same eve and vented every ounce at him. It shrunk my spirit with regret. I was wrong. I could not be gentle like my father. I had been a beast myself.

I rolled my shoulders to face them. Lethia snored softly. Kenter's eyes held mine for a brief moment. He was awake, too. It was evident he was exhausted and his horrid wounds would need mending. What had I been thinking to leave the bloody mess alone to him last night? I'd been wrong to do it. He said nothing, but instead rose to go outside. The air was thick with anticipation as to what would happen this morning.

I thought to a long lesson from Tarron as I started a pot of water for our tea. As soon as Kenter returned, I took my turn outside. It had rained while we slept. The wet grass stuck to my feet as I stepped out into the great green world, carrying a burden this morn. The pit in my stomach did not leave when I gathered eggs or searched to retrieve the healing herbs I dropped last night on my way to the house. As I closed the door upon my return, Lethia sat stretching the night away with her arms.

"Good morn," she said softly.

"Good morn," I replied quieter than usual.

~ ~ ~

Carmella rested on my shoulder while

I prepared breakfast. I would let the foods have a turn on the counter before we ate. I had to release this burden of weight now, here, this morning.

I brought the cups of tea to the bedding, handed them each theirs, and sat down before them. Their eyes held caution of the telling of my words, even before I spoke them.

"I will be the first to say my thoughts this morn," I said calmly.

If I sounded confident, it was the opposite of what my heart spoke. But I would do as Tarron had trained me to do. Sincerity of spirit is vital. I had to tell them my feelings and thoughts about last night's incident with the bear. I was terrified they would not accept my apology, but none the less, they both deserved it.

Lethia's fingers dug nervously into the soft comfort of her blanket. Kenter's expression reminded me of a frustrated child I once watched a professor scold. His eyes viewed the floor as if deep in thought, his jaw showing clenched teeth. I wasn't the only one feeling unnerved as the two sat awaiting my next words.

"Last night was not good. Lethia should not have gone outside alone," I said, looking directly into her eyes as she stared back. "Not at night. Not yet. You are too new to this place," I said dropping my gaze. "And she should not have left the door open. It draws the bear nearer. He knows it as an entryway into our world that he cannot otherwise pursue."

I forced myself to ignore the tears that fell from Lethia's eyes. My words were important, and I needed to finish them without tears of my own interfering.

"I know this concerning the door, because I have done it myself, more than once. The second time I left it open, the bear was in the hillhouse all night while I hid in the smokehouse tunnel that I'd started to dig to store roots for the winter. The tunnel was smaller then, and angled to a slant. I could hardly hold my space in it without keeping hold of roots. It rained on that night, too.

"It was a fierce storm that shook the Earth with its thunder. Lightning shot through the sky for hours. I could not go outside, or to the trees to escape him, or even to watch him from that distance, for fear of the lightening reaching me there.

The whole night I waited, shivering

in that sloping tunnel, in the cold of the smokehouse.

"I was terrified I would fall asleep and roll out of it and he would break the door and come claw me, and bite me, and have me for his breakfast. I feared that those who swam the Pool of Light next would enter this world and not find me. My greatest fear was that none would know what became of me. I would simply perish into the stomach of that bear.

"As I huddled in the smokehouse, he ate the food in the house, broke useful things, and ruined and stole the only blanket I had. Then as I feared, he came looking for me at the break of day.

"Since the tunnel was surrounded by thick tree trunks and roots, he could not get to me, but the smokehouse walls were not secured into the ground. He broke them with his anger, entered, and tried to reach me in the dug-out with his sharp claws. You see what he has left of that place. Then he ate my smoked meat.

"I was left alive, but with little to eat, nothing for warmth. You are not alone in this lesson, Lethia. As I spoke before, we cannot leave the door open at night. I am sorry I was not here when you went out and that I did not tell this story before."

While they sat stunned, I sipped at my tea. My words stood firm upon her ears and I was glad. Kenter was next. He turned to listen as I spoke. Unlike Lethia, he sat solid, eyes unmoved.

"Kenter, while I do not believe that we'll agree on the methods we each used last night, you will hear from me now. I am sorry for shouting at you. Know though, that I meant what I said. When you have been in this place for three years, you may feel differently about methods of safety. You should have stayed in this house. But I know you love your sister. What you did was brave, but foolish. I will not be as surprised the next time I see that from you, the bravery, I mean. But my shouting at you, I hope we can mend our anger."

Kenter took in my words for only a moment before he spoke.

"I'm not angry, now." He glared at me. "But know this, no matter what words escape your lips, or what you and that bear have done in the past, I will never leave either of you in the dark with a beast. No matter what your words say."

His dark eyes dared me to break the stare.

"No matter what your words say," he repeated more harshly. "So do not expect it. Do not think it," he said slowly. "I am the first male and protector."

For the longest moment, we both refused to drop our eyes. Then the sores upon his face screamed for my attention. They were scabbed and horrid.

Kenter was still angry, no matter what *his* words said. But, I could not be surprised. Had it been Tarron outside in the dark with the bear, or either of the twins for that matter, I would not have stayed in the hillhouse, either.

It was my job to be protector at the moment and I felt I knew best, the safest means for us all. I had learned safety. He had not. He was not ready to fight a beast, especially in his condition. But, I would teach him all I could about safety over the next moon cycle, so the weight of the burden did not sit upon my shoulders alone. He would be healed by then. Lethia was tender. She was not like us. Not yet, anyway. I looked again at his wounded face. Along with the bandages, he had torn off whole strips of skin from around the edges of his face last night, leaving small chunks of flesh missing from his cheeks. The results were numerous thick and bubbly scabs. He would have most terrible scars from it. His face would never look the same as before he swam.

He'd done it so he could see better in his attempt to save us from the bear. He'd endured much pain in order to keep us safe, at least in his mind, and he had thought to save us both.

Perhaps I had misjudged Kenter's strength… and his selfishness.

Chapter Seventeen

Though still covered with bandages, Kenter's skin was nearly healed. They hadn't seen the bear since that night. Except for the soft yellow glow of the small lamp, it was pitch black out tonight, but for the grasses on which they stood. Those were alit with tiny lights that flittered about.

"Fireflies or lightning bugs, not sun flies," Tolomay corrected Kenter.

He threw his hand up and turned to face her.

"Like it makes a grand difference! If you remember your trainings so well, why did you not log these things down?" he barked. "Butterflies... Flutterbyes, who cares? Three years seems plenty of time to write a guide book, Tolomay. Just think it. You would have had full journal notes by now!" he yelled.

He was annoyed; he was very

annoyed. The female thought it that just because she was the first, she knew everything about everything in this place. She felt the need to correct his every mistake. It was as if Professor Maxy himself had followed him here. He thought she could have put better teaching methods to use. But rather than help him find the precious Juper, or give him something to read, she chose to lead him from place to place explaining things to him as if he were a two-year-old child. She thought he was stupid. He was not. He was brilliant, well trained and at the top of his class.

And what of it that he hadn't remembered the word window? Did it really matter? Who here cared? After all, he'd not seen one before entering the clean world, and he seemed to survive through life just fine without that one stupid word.

Learning of buildings and their parts was Lethia's expertise, not his. He did not care of it. The environment back home had deteriorated so quickly since Tolomay's swim that the windows and doors at the pod communities had been permanently sealed shut with metal walls to keep the solar flares out.

It happened before he was even born. No one was allowed outside. Tolomay was ridiculous. Outside had not existed in his world since solar radiation pierced holes in the ozone. Even then, solar flares had penetrated two other pod communities, killing most of those citizens, including a candidate he and Lethia knew.

The only window he'd seen, had been the cathedral ceiling glass that had been uncovered for their swim and that was called a skylight, not a window. How could he know of such things? Now he had to hear the same criticism from her about misspeaking the term sun bug?

It bothered him she expected so much. His strength was returning and he was feeling almost his old self again, even better than himself. He was feeling fully male. He no longer needed her pity, or her self-righteous lessons.

Holding Carmella, Lethia sat silently on a log and watched the two of them once again arguing. She was growing tired of their bickering and really, her brother had a point. She and Kenter could not remember everything as easily as Tolomay knew it. Unlike her, they did not have photographic minds, and they hadn't been trained in all the same subjects. The pod library had suffered a fire since she swam. It left fewer books available at the candidates' disposal than when Tolomay lived there, and the twins had always needed to study to learn.

Tolomay had no idea of her brother's brilliance when it came to metals and certain other subjects. He was above average intelligence in trainings that were quite difficult for most, knowledge of solar energy, electronics, electricity and mechanics. Those things came naturally to him. Dealing with them was more effortless to him than for many of the professors who taught him.

But here he had no equipment to use. If only they had found the Juper. But these lessons of outdoors things, he simply had no interest. It did no good for Tolomay to walk them about from the grasses to the trees, explaining what her brother did not care to learn and would so soon forget.

Kenter was not interested in Tolomay's lessons of outdoor creatures and plant life. That was why he'd grown bored and rarely studied those subjects, even as Mize Maxy himself taught him.

Had they found the Juper, and thus the buried supplies, Kenter could have shown Tolomay what he was truly capable of, his use in making items which would prove important to each of them and everyone to come into the clean world.

His contributions would greatly ease their workload. But the Juper had been lost. Without it, they could not find the metals and supplies he needed for his expertise. He could not help their community. Not yet, but that wasn't *his* fault. Lethia wanted to tell Tolomay how brilliant he was, but she was not his parent, and at present the two were arguing. It was not the time for those words. A solution to their problem would be best.

Tolomay was furious. How dare this male, who could not last a day on his own in the clean world shout at her again! Without her assistance, the scarring on his hands could have possibly maimed him for life. Just because he was the only male here didn't give him the privilege to treat her as if he were the parent. And worse, Tarron had never once raised his voice to her. She was growing tired of it. Males should not speak to females in such a manner and she for one would not keep mum about it. Kenter acted like he didn't even *want* to learn things. He seemed contented to sit on the bedding that she had pieced together for him before he even arrived, while his sister catered to his every whim.

"The two of them are well suited as siblings," Tolomay thought. "He's the king, and she, his sklavo." Lethia did too much for him. The only time he'd shown an inkling of effort himself had been the incident with the bear, and that had been adrenalin ruling his arms. Even at that, his healing afterward had to begin anew.

Well, Tolomay was not Lethia and he better learn that fact if they were to get along at all. She could not help that she had a photographic memory and wasn't in the habit of writing. It's not that she couldn't write, but she'd never needed to take notes on the things she was taught. She learned something once, and simply remembered it.

"A book *would* help," Lethia interjected in almost an apology.

Tolomay ignored her, but scooped

Carmela up from the female's lap before turning to Kenter.

"You're not even trying," she said under her breath and stormed off toward the hillhouse. A few steps away, she could no longer hold her tongue. The grass beneath her feet squealed their burn, as she spun around for one last jab at him.

"If you want pen and paper and notes, then put yourself to task and get them made," she said. "*You* make a journal. *You* take the writings. I am not your sklavo!"

Then she stopped abruptly, set down the lantern, and disappeared into the dark. Sister and brother exchanged a stare. Kenter was baffled.

"What's a sklavo?" he asked Lethia.

"I think it's something to do with wait staff, depending too much on another. Or it's work as another's servant, without choice or reward, something in that arena. As if a captive," she replied. "Don't worry, brother. She won't stay mad."

That's what Tolomay thought of him? She was his captive? How could she think that when he and Lethia were captive to *her* commands?

He raised his chin and turned to Lethia. What did his sister mean, she won't stay mad? He was the one who was mad. He couldn't help but be angry with Tolomay when she knew so much more than he did about this world.

Kenter tried to exercise patience, but his emotions were stealing the best of him away. Whenever he was around her, all he could think to was those shining blue eyes. He could barely take in her words at all. It wasn't his fault that her striking eyes and the movement of her body captivated more of his thoughts than her words did lately.

"Sklavo… humph," he said.

Little did she know. He did not depend too much on others, was capable, and knew a great many things. As the first male he was the best trained in his fields of expertise; everyone knew this.

Kenter thought about the day. When they awoke, the females had served breakfast. In fact they'd served all the food, and Tolomay had caught the food since he and Lethia had arrived, but she had been choosing it. She was good at hunting and was fast. It was logical. That wasn't Kenter's fault, nor was it his fault he had been injured during transport.

How could she not see his contributions today, telling Tolomay which food tasted best and listening to her words, as distracting as she was? He even made her laugh a time or two and had walked at least a mile with them, the last of it excruciating on his pain filled legs, since the burns healing on his ankles had split and bled this morning. He hadn't mentioned it to either of them. He was trying, wasn't he?

It was Tolomay's fault they argued, not his. He was used to the females back home catering to him, trying to please him, wanting his attention. Something was clearly wrong with her. She did none of these things. And, she was stubborn; when he got angry, she got angry back.

Kenter growled his frustration into the night, until his sister quickly reminded him of the beasts.

His fingers were drawn to his face.

"And this!" he complained as he rubbed his cheek ferociously, through the bandage. "She tells me to leave it on, as if *she* feels this itch all day!"

He didn't have to take orders from

her. He reached up to remove it, but Lethia's words stopped him.

"She's right, Kenter. Leave it to heal," she said firmly.

He abided, but now the dangling piece of the bandage he'd loosened tickled his cheek even more. He rubbed the spot again to stop the new itch and tucked it back in place. He thought to rip every last bandage off, no matter the female's words. It was his face! His hands! He was the male! He could do what he liked!

And then it happened. What he saw next made a change in his mind that would not step itself back.

Kenter noticed the lantern Tolomay deposited near him as it whispered its soft yellow glow to his feet. She'd left it in order the two would not get lost on the trip home. He knew with all certainty that had been her thinking.

She would know her way in the dark. The twins would not. That realization stopped him. He picked it up and stared at the stone in the center of its top.

The female had somehow found a way to bore a small hole through the center of the stone, to give place for a wick to slip through, to keep the flame away from the clay bowl that carried the oil. He wondered how she had done it. Had she ground it out with a sharp stone? Perhaps she'd searched in the stream for weeks, to find one that bragged a hole in it. He viewed the attached willow handle. How long had it taken a thirteen year old to design and make this one single lamp, and yet he used it all this while without a thought to the task involved. She was much more patient than he; he was much more selfish.

Then Kenter did something he'd not thought it to do. He put himself in the female's situation. "How did she feel about today?" he wondered. He thought about the tasks she had accomplished and Lethia's tasks, too, the food gathering, the cooking, the digging of a new fire pit, the fetching of water and the washing. He could not believe it. Tolomay was right.

The females *had* been doing all the work. He had been lazy. It suddenly dawned on him his sister always did much of his work, even when he was not injured. This was an instant awareness that washed over him like a rainfall. It left him feeling weak.

He wondered why his twin had done so much for him on a continuous basis. It was no wonder Tolomay did not view him as the strong male he was. She'd seen only the things he did not do. She did not know him at all. He was so capable, and of such greater things.

He determined it at that very moment and would not expect Tolomay to be his sklavo. He set it in his mind to make amends with her and to make ink, pen and paper tomorrow. He would gather the supplies himself, would take his own notes, start a journal, and write the training books for others. He could be the male Tolomay needed him to be.

"Come on," he said to Lethia, as he picked up the lantern. "Let's go home," and the two strode through the grasses, toward the hillhouse that Tolomay built.

Chapter Eighteen

The sun brushed their faces with its gentle heat as the grasses blew in the breeze, tickling their legs. Lethia and Kenter were near one another doing separate tasks. Kenter wrapped while Lethia plucked. They sat upon their hill, with Tolomay a stone's throw away.

Kenter counted in his head and continued wrapping the leather tie... "twenty-four...twenty-five...twenty-six." Once he reached twenty seven turns, he knotted the ends as Tolomay had shown him, but not tightly enough. The result was two sticks bound together to make one long straight pole, but the top portion wobbled as he shook it. The bandages on his hands now covered only his palms and still, they got in his way. He would have to re-wrap the whole thing... again.

"Didn't Mize say this place was once the United World's Land, Leth. Wasn't it?" he asked.

He watched Tolomay's delicate hands wrapping her own strappings. She wasn't even listening to him today. He couldn't help himself staring at her lips.

"Yes," his sister answered. "This is where the merging of the Mericas was the first attempt of the GoldHoarders to unite nations in order to control citizens," his sister answered. "After their weather machines wreaked disaster, they deliberately crippled the economy through use of a one world currency. Once citizens felt desperate enough, they were enticed by the idea a government would take care of them. By the time they realized they were being exterminated by their own senate representatives, it was too late. It's ironic really, and strange, to think it that the land here turned into the first death trap. It began as the freest of all nations, one of hopes and dreams and freedoms."

Lethia paused for a moment to enjoy the glorious meadow where they all three sat.

"But the GoldHoarders lost in the end," she finished. "They all perished."

Brother and sister held each other's

somber glance. Lethia broke it to look back at the tail feathers she was plucking from the hind of a stiff, dead bird. They were making bows and arrows for hunting, and fishing poles.

Tolomay sat ten paces away, and was winding straps onto her own sticks. She could wrap arrows and fishing poles without thought. Too busy remembering, she said nothing.

~ ~ ~

The sun was out and it shown through the lab window, lighting the room brighter than usual. She spent half her waking hours in this room, learning from Tarron. Even at five years old, she felt this was unusual, though she was just beginning to realize the extent of it. None of the other children trained nearly as much as Tarron trained her. Sitting in the light, she wondered.

"Father, why does my skin and hair speak of light?" she asked.

She looked very different than all others in the community and she did not want to. She was the only citizen without brown or black hair and they wore darker skin and eyes. While they closely resembled photos she'd seen of American Indian ancients, she resembled no one.

Even Tarron himself was black haired, brown skinned and black eyed. She felt she did not belong. Her only distraction from that feeling was to keep busy, which was why she liked her father teaching her in his lab. But even that reminded her that she did not fit in. No other child she knew was gifted with home tutoring, at their simple request, whenever it suited them. She felt it was offered to her so none would be forced to view her.

No one mentioned her ghostly coloring. The community rules forbade cruelty, but she sometimes heard the whispers of other children in the eating room. It wasn't just the children.

Recently, while sitting near the entrance to the chamber room, she overheard senate council members speaking of her in a way that unnerved her. She did not recognize all their words, but felt strongly they disapproved of her.

They mentioned her father, and that she had been his *wrong choice* and that she had *kissed his shoes*. She loved her father, but why had they thought it she'd kissed his shoes? She'd never done that. That was weeks ago but she had not asked Tarron about it. For some reason, the subject seemed taboo, but this morning's incident at training prompted her to ask questions.

During recess, after history class, one of the males in the classroom drew Tolomay's inch long hair through his fingers. A seven-year-old female gasped at the sight. Clearly annoyed and disgusted by the act, she pushed his hand from Tolomay's head. As Tolomay was left to rub away the sting of pulled hair, the two ran off laughing to play. She found herself once again alone. Her thoughts dwelt on today's history lesson.

Tarron answered her question of her hair and skin coloring.

"You are unique in that you carry the DNA of another community," he said. "That makes you special, Tolomay."

She sat silent. She did not want to be special.

His words did not help the feeling of loneliness, which lived deep inside her belly. She knew Tarron loved her. She was, after all, one of only a handful in the community who *had* a parent; unlike the other children raised by the community as a whole, her father was always there for her personally. She had more love than the others because of it, but still, she was different, even from him. Her gaze dropped to the floor.

"You are no different than any community member. We are each unique, and you are a most unique child. Our differences, what separates us from one another, is what makes us able to see through individual eyes. Yours happen to be blue."

Tolomay held her silence, so Tarron stepped to where she sat.

"I will tell you about the day you were born," he said, sitting beside her on the wide plastic window box. "I think it that you are of an age old enough to hear this. I was present when you arrived. I delivered you from your mother's womb, the last infant grown from the inner body. You were the last natural birth, Tolomay, before lab births were mandated due to dietary risks. Imagine the glorious energy in that," he spoke in awe. "Forming cells and growing limbs inside an actual womb."

She reached up and touched her father's hair. It was so nicely textured. Hers grew too thin. He rubbed his hand over her stubble of blond and then drew it down to the side of her cheek. Resting his fingertips beneath her chin, he tilted her face upward in order to catch her gaze with his dark and knowing eyes.

"It was your mother whose hair was golden like the sun and eyes as blue as the sky. That is why you have them, her DNA. She was beautiful and you look just like her."

She smiled weakly and Tarron released her chin.

Stepping from her, he left the room, only to return moments later with a small folded piece of waxy paper in his hand. He un-wrapped it and set the flat square into her hand. It looked similar to a brown plastic playing piece from her school games, but was covered with a mysterious white powdery substance.

"I've been saving that for you since the day you were born," said her father.

Tolomay stared at it.

"It's for tasting, as a celebration treat," he explained.

"Like a fruit?" she asked.

It looked nothing like a fruit.

Tarron did not answer, but rather motioned toward her mouth so she would try it. He was excited for her. She set it between her lips and bit at one piece of corner.

"If you let it settle on your tongue, it will melt into something quite wondrous."

Tolomay did, and her eyes smiled to match her lips. She sat silent as it finished its turn on her tongue and she swallowed the last of it down.

"That's called chocolate, Tolomay, and it is our secret. We can study it tomorrow, if you'd like."

"Thank you, father."

Tarron knew his child. Her thoughts were still distant. Whatever was on her mind weighed so heavy on her heart, even the last available piece of chocolate did not ease her.

"Something distresses you," he said. "What is it?"

She was seldom uncomfortable asking Tarron anything. She felt this subject was expected to be left unbroached. Even still, every photograph in history class screamed the question out to her. She had no choice.

"Was my mother a GoldHoarder?" she blurted in barely a whisper.

Tarron's eyes painted a fleeting expression that terrified her. No matter his answer, something was horrid about her mother and her as well. She watched the effect of her question as her words cut him like a knife. She had never seen Tarron scared and her heart raced with her own fear of it.

A long silence prefaced his response, then he cleared his throat and knelt. Gently touching her shoulder, his eyes held hers with a grave sincerity.

"Tolomay, you must never repeat those words to anyone," was all he said. "Outside of training, none need speak of GoldHoarders."

His words confirmed her suspicions. Even Tarron's love for her could not erase the fact she was different and something was very wrong with her. Everyone could see it. She could not hide her skin and eyes, even when her hair was shaved. She would have to work harder than anyone just to feel a member of her community, so that they would not all hate her as the elder in the hall who called her a *wrong choice*.

She would become the most

knowledgeable. She did, after all, remember her lessons verbatim. That was a manner in which she did not mind being different. It would help her to be of use to others, so she could belong.

"Tolomay, do you understand me?" Tarron's dark eyes stared at her. "Tolomay?"

"Tolomay!" Kenter shouted as the stone he threw landed on the grasses near her foot. It brought her thoughts instantly back to the present with a quiet *thump*.

She stared at him and blinked. As funny as he occasionally was, Kenter could be so irritating.

"I called you three times," he said. "Where were you?"

"Nowhere," she replied, and then saw his tangled project. "That's a mess! What have you done to those poor sticks?"

Her sturdy pole bounced slightly as she released it to the ground and stood to retrieve his wobbly sticks from him. She examined them and made adjustments, standing so close to him that he took in her smell. Her flower oils were tantalizing. Squeezing the two rods together, she handed them back.

"Like this," she said, showing him where to match up the grooves in the wood. "Unwrap it and try again."

"Right," Kenter said, irritated she all but ignored him today.

Lethia's bird was half bare as she drew a feather down the side of her cheek. A pile of others lay upon large leaves beside her. Tolomay smiled.

"That's good, Lethia. More than enough," she said. "We will leave the rest to the Earth."

She handed the sister two sticks and strapping.

"I'll teach you both fishing tomorrow."

"What's your opinion of it, Tolomay?" Lethia asked. "Do you think it possible the GoldHoarders left anything of use in this ground beneath us?"

Lethia was learning to stay out of Tolomay and Kenter's arguments and Tolomay was beginning to think of her as a sister. She loved Lethia very much. She did not want to be cruel by telling her she should not speak of things as evil as GoldHoarders. The last thing Tolomay wanted to converse of just now was things buried in the ground.

She selected two good branches from the pile, pulled more strapping from the basket, and this time sat closer to the twins, as she began wrapping another pole.

"Where's Carmella?" she said, avoiding Lethia's question all together.

Chapter Nineteen

Tolomay slept fitfully. Though Lethia slept beside her, the sister did not rouse. From across the room Kenter watched Tolomay, who whined briefly, then turned to his direction. She was sound asleep. The embers from the fire were almost out, but in the dim light he could still see her. She was breathtaking; her lips and face perfect as could be. It was hard to believe someone so stubborn could look so heavenly while asleep. She rolled over and out of his view. He watched the ceiling beams fade in the small and tired flame.

Tolomay was like a storm, unpredictable and stronger than one might expect, full of lightning and thunder. But she was also as calm, and aged, and refreshing as the stream after the rain passed. She had a gentleness of spirit, a kindness, and lovingness about her that showed more often than not. But her spirit held a strength that could not be defined.

It was only when frustrated she would show that power to lash out in anger. Although he did not care for that side of her, when it reared itself up, she was quick to discard it. She was fast to forgive and more generous than most citizens he had known, but she was steady.

She knew her worth of it, and her place here. She knew when she faltered and she knew when she was right. But her greatest attribute was how much she loved the clean world. She had a pure heart toward it, almost as if she breathed in all life in this place.

He could easily see why she had been chosen first to enter this paradise. She was a far better candidate than he, though he would never speak it. He thought her amazing, stubbornness and all, and had a plan of it. He would find a way to make her see him for who he really was, not the male who'd been burned so badly he became needy in the wake of arriving in this place.

He felt more himself as each day

passed and had spent long weeks preparing mentally for the things he would contribute to their group…once he was well. Except for the night of the bear, he wasn't able to do much physically between his hands and feet healing and the pain of his skin, especially after the healing had to begin once again on that eve. But that was some time ago and he improved, even tremendously improved, over the last handful of days. He was back, healthy.

He'd been feeling his face for the past hour and touched at it again. Barely hurting now, the skin was much smoother without the bandages leaving their textured ripples rubbing upon tender flesh. Tolomay said he no longer needed the wound sap and aloe, but some of the scars would remain forever. He was glad they weren't worse. What if she found him unattractive, too unattractive? Did she think him hideous because of them?

Perhaps that was why she'd ignored his face this eve. But no, it was as if she saw right through him to the other side of the room when she removed the bandages.

She had been more interested in inspecting the color of the scabs in the firelight and the goo that remained on his dressings, and then the feel of his scarring, than of viewing the results of her curation, which was to look upon his face and see him, eye to eye. Tonight, she made him feel invisible. He did not understand how someone like Tolomay could see everything except him.

She was just guarded, he decided, and thinks only of the tasks that await their turn with her. He guessed it was from solitude that she was this way or perhaps from the pain of separation when she arrived in this world alone. It was as though she felt a burden for the entirety of survival itself. Was the cause of it her sorrow? To have all those you know ripped from you would be tragic to the heart.

At the same time it was that which made her so different than all females he'd known. A female who survived alone so long in a strange world would not plead and grovel and bend her spirit to be with a male. She would accept no less than an equal as a partner and he realized it.

He could help her, and teach and lead her at times, but he had to be willing to allow her lead when necessary, without his pride standing in the way.

That was his predicament, and his problem. It was difficult for him to follow another's feet. He was always racing to be first. At the least of it, he knew it. He guessed she wanted that from him though, for him to be her equal and walk beside her, perhaps offer arms of comfort when she needed them. No matter how strong she was, she was still a female after all, and all females wanted that.

He felt certain that given time, he could win her interest and then she could learn to depend on him, but first he needed to find the Juper and supplies. They all needed them. He closed his eyes, listening to the night sounds. He had searched out every inch of the grasses to no avail. Perhaps they *had* lost it in the Pool of Light.

"Tarron," Tolomay whispered, as if in pain, and then gasped softly. He heard her turn. She was dreaming, still.

~ ~ ~

In her dream, Tarron stood on a mountain of stone. A large hawk flew above him cawing loudly. He watched it with adoration until suddenly, it dropped its wing to thrust Tarron from the cliff. He fell silently, without so much as a scream. It woke her. The pit of her stomach ached. She saw the coals were almost out, and knew she would be unable to sleep just now, after that nightmare.

It took a few moments for the embers to grab at the log she placed onto them, until slowly, it came alive with flame. She hoped it would not disturb the others. Lethia remained asleep, but then Tolomay noticed Kenter's stare.

"You should go back to sleep," she said softly.

"I haven't been asleep," he remarked. "I was thinking."

It dawned on Tolomay he had watched her start the fire.

"About what?'

"The hillhouse," he answered.

He couldn't tell her the truth.

"What of it?"

"Now that my hands are healed, I can help build Lethia's design. We will have more inside space."

Tolomay soaked in the thought. It

would be strange to live in a different home, but hers was too small for all of them. They covered nearly a third of its entirety just to lay the blankets to sleep.

"If we could connect hers to the hillhouse, it would prove safest, against the bear," she replied.

"Yes," he remarked, staring at her.

She was so beautiful. Lethia turned her face to the two and blinked.

"What are you talking?" she asked.

"Your new house," Kenter answered, nonchalantly before she snorted and closed her eyes.

Tolomay smiled at him.

"She won't remember in the morn," he said. "She talks in her sleep, sometimes."

Tolomay laughed under her breath then poked at the fire with a stick. She breathed deeply.

"I *love* the sound and smell of the flames," she said, turning to him.

"The first element studied," Kenter replied, though he was certain that she knew.

Tolomay raised her brows. He could read the interest in her eyes. Had she not studied this subject?

"By the ancients in the science

fields," he added. "For every society, fire was the first to be studied... in the sciences... in chemistry, after alchemy initially failed a solution."

Tolomay had *not* trained in this area, and she *never* heard Kenter explain training to her. She waited for him to continue. This was a new experience.

"The study of fire led to the discovery of glass and purification of metals. Without fire, neither would exist... nor would have man mined gold, though, and look at the result of it."

Tolomay knew what he meant. Without gold there would have been no riches, no GoldHoarders killing off society and the Earth.

"But those types would have found another means of destruction, even without it," he concluded, almost reading her thoughts.

She nodded in agreement and Kenter continued.

"Metallurgy is one of my main fields. I've trained extensively. The first time, it brought upon the original Bronze Age. Now, I am to make one here. That's my purpose."

He paused. Should he stop? Was she

bored with his knowledge yet? After all, he had no photographic memory and unlike her, he had trained extensively in only a handful of subjects. She remained quiet, as if in wait. Perhaps she was not yet bored.

"The original Bronze age began in Eurasia," he continued. "My task is to start the first metal age for the clean world, but more modern... to design useful metals, tools, equipment for the future of all. When the time comes and we find the Juper, I can use the precious metals. And glass is buried for us as well, for my solar panels for...uh..."

Tolomay's intense and beautiful stare distracted his thoughts before he found them again.

"To ease the work in the house. All that we do will be made easier," he said, "...now that I am healed."

Kenter's shared knowledge of his training left her speechless. All this time she assumed he was sent here merely for his physical strength, for construction, to assist Lethia and her with the tools he'd spoken of making once he healed. But she thought their tools would be constructed of wood and rock. She knew nothing of this metallurgy field he now spoke of. She was almost angry at him for not telling her earlier, but remained in such surprise of it, that her anger rained to her feet before it could rise up. His eyes held a calmer assurance now than she had ever seen.

"Why have you not spoken of this?" she asked.

"Why would I?" he replied. "I have not found the Juper. I have no supplies. Without them, my knowledge is useless."

Then he viewed her directly, with a look she could not read.

"And… you never asked," he said. "You've been busy teaching us what to eat and how to fight against bears… how to garden and fish and hunt…how to survive," he paused before continuing. "You sometimes task yourself with too much thinking on it, Tolomay: surviving. Do not forget to live it as well."

Tolomay was humbled. Though she disagreed and knew survival was the most important thing, she chose not to argue because she saw him in a new light and was anxious to know more. He was not stupid after all. He had studied things Tarron had not taught her. Why had she not asked him of this before, more of himself and *his* extensive trainings? Her dumbfounded look eventually found his eyes and a smile crept up one side of his mouth. He was happy and relaxed. His arrogance left him the moment he spoke of metallurgy.

She thought to it. There was much more to Kenter than hot-headedness, muscles, and a pair of hands, and she had only now fully realized it. He would not be a burden to their community, but perhaps rather an asset, metals aside. She looked to his scars. They shone brightly in the light, but he had healed well.

His stomach growled.

"Are you hungry?" she asked.

"Starving," he said matter-of-factly, then rose to a stand. "I'll help."

Tolomay stared at him through a moment, and then answered in a challenge.

"All right," she said. "let's see if you can cook with this fire of yours."

Tolomay's World and The Pool of Light

ChapTer Twenty

I'd never eaten mid-eve with another. The pod community had sleeping rules, and none were allowed the freedom of the kitchen, not even Tarron. Food was served during eating schedules and seldom was more than a snack provided in one's pod room.

This was much more fun and Kenter and I cooked it together. He was without a clue as to how to cook, which made me laugh. No matter his mistakes, he took them with stride. I supposed it was his great pride that allowed it, but I did not mind. It harmonized the experience for both of us. When he broke the eggs, we had to spend minutes afterwards, in the dim light of the fire, picking the shells from the bowl where they lay mingled with the gooey insides.

While cutting an onion he cried like an infant. His idea of seasoning an omelet was to pour entirely too much of all the herbs into it without a thought as to breaking up any of them first. Still, the food turned out amazingly well. He slipped in some newt carrot chunks as a surprise, when I stepped outside briefly. It added a crunchy texture that felt good on my tongue. I never would have used carrots, but they offered their sweet flavor, and it was good.

We ate until our stomachs were heavy, laughing quietly throughout much of the meal. Kenter's newly discovered smile warmed my heart. His lips turned up a slight bit more on one side when he smiled, but they suited his face and his straight and perfect teeth. Then a thought struck me I'd not thought of before, not even while pulling off his bandages, for I had been focused on his wounds and healing at the time, and not him, never him, not really.

Sitting here now in this light and having a real conversation brought a realization to my mind; it was a fact I had neglected to see in my frustration concerning his ignorance of this world that was so new to him. To my view, Kenter was quite remarkably handsome, even with his scars. He caught my thought in his eye, and my embarrassment forced me to turn away.

I would guard myself from this path. I was still the protector and would need to maintain my position until a reason presented itself for me to think otherwise. I could not yet grow attached to this male. Not in the way my heart urged me to in this moment. I knew of things they did not. I would not allow his choice of me yet, though I felt in his great warmth at that moment, he might lean toward the thought of it.

Still, spending time with Kenter alone, while Lethia slept, brought us much closer. Neither wore stubbornness on our shoulders this eve. Perhaps exhaustion caused us to drop our guard.

While we visited, I felt carefree as a small child. It was refreshing to my heart. His spirit brushed at mine with its heat. For the first time since I could remember, I had no fear of some task being out in the world that I was missing to do.

I had no concerns of waiting for others to come, no worries I would perish, leaving others to arrive wondering what had become of me. For the first time since leaving Tarron, I was truly at peace and happy.

We sat for hours. I was so engaged in his funny childhood stories and our laughter, I soon forgot there was more to the world than only the two of us. Then, unexpectedly, he reached toward my cheek and drew his fingers through my shoulder length locks.

"The sunlight lives in your hair," he said in adoration.

Chills shot down my arms as I gazed deep into his eyes. It was the only time in my existence, my hair did not cause me shame. My thoughts were far from thinking of my mother and the possibility that she'd been a GoldHoarder.

Carmella broke the moment when she crawled across the table and helped herself to a drink. Kenter's smile stopped my heart and my lips could do nothing but reply with one of their own. The whole while he had been here I had missed him beneath the bandages. I was glad he'd been set free. For the first time since they'd arrived, I felt I could know him without anger and frustration taking its place between our feet.

ChapTer Twenty One

It was four times now we'd been to the hill to await the arrival of others. Kenter and Lethia said the Vision Fold's plan was to launch candidates twice a month through the Pool of Light, but as of yet, not one had arrived. It had been eight weeks.

We were all hungry for dinner. It was clear they would not come today. I was halfway done brushing Lethia's dark silky hair with the new brush we took turns to make. The thin wooden stubs for bristles on mine had completed their three year turn for a purpose. Kenter disposed of it in the fire.

"I cannot believe we have to wait here so long, every other Tuesday," he said in complaint. "It's the worst,"

"Yes," I answered. "I know."

For a moment, it sounded like he was comparing our group of three, waiting a measly four times within two moon cycles, to me waiting alone one hundred and eighty eight times in three years. Just days ago I would have barked a response at him. But now, I knew he didn't mean that. Still, a look of feeling foolish hung on his face for a sweeping moment until he righted his comment.

"I don't know how you did it," he said staring at me so profoundly I felt the warmth of his spirit stir deep within my soul.

"You're the strongest person I have ever known," he finished.

Heart quivering, my cheeks reddened instantly. It almost brought water to my eyes. I stopped brushing for a moment. I did not know what to say. The power of the feeling terrified me; still, I did not turn away from his compliment, or his magnetic stare.

Lethia noticed his depth of conviction. She peered up from the flowers she was weaving, which drew Kenter's attention away from my eyes, to hers. Too proud to allow his embarrassment, he dropped his gaze to the tree line and one at a time threw the few small rocks from his hand, into the woods. His step followed. I was sure he would search for it again.

The brush pulled at Lethia's hair as she turned back to her task, but said nothing. Lethia was a listener. She often said nothing. When she did speak, her words were soft. Unlike Kenter and me, a shout had likely never breached her lips.

Kind hearted and quite reasonable, Lethia was the glue of the three of us. She learned quickly that getting involved in an argument between Kenter and me caused problems for us all. Unless she felt strongly about an issue, and not simply that she needed to defend her brother, she more often than not let us battle it out between ourselves. I think she knew it that I was as stubborn as he, and logicked if she allowed that trait in him, she would allow it in me. I was part of their community too, and she cared for me.

Above all else, Lethia preferred peace and so had a way of speaking her mind when it mattered to her. Kenter and I had much respect for the times *our* sister stepped in. When that happened, we both turned our ears to her.

To me she was more than a sister.

She was like a mother, but not one to take care of me; she was not a protector, but rather one who listened when I needed to shed matters of my heart to another female. Neither of us had a mother or sister and so we both greatly enjoyed each other's support.

Lethia and Kenter agreed on much and the bond between twins was strong. But surprisingly, on a few occasions Lethia took her agreement to my side and made it clear to Kenter that he needed more thought on the subject at hand. At times though, my ears heard the very same things. She was a holder of logic which amazed me for someone so tender as she.

Despite her mannerism and because of it, she could never be a leader and no matter at that. Though Kenter was the first male, he knew little of the clean world, so my word was generally adhered to.

Little by little, I allowed them more input into the decisions made. After all, we were a community and in a community everyone's opinion should be heard. As long as all were fed, and healthy and safe, my ears were open to suggestions. For the lesser things, everyone's input was considered and we decided together; still, I had final say. Kenter stepped into the thick trees and out of sight.

"Lethia," I said.

"Yes."

"Why does he place such importance in finding this Juper of his?"

Lethia waited until the brush left the strands before she turned her head toward me.

"It offers real riches, Tolomay. He is right to be diligent in finding it. These are treasures we can each use here."

I bit my lip. I loathed treasures. Treasures were what the GoldHoarders worshipped. They had been used in order to kill off humanity as best they could before Earth paid them in karma.

"We do not need them. The Earth is our treasure here," I answered.

"No, Tolomay. The treasures it offers are of metal and glass from the earth, not ones of hoarding and killing. These are for natural sustenance's. Kenter is proficient in their use. He needs them. We all do."

I nodded, though I did not believe any of the three of us needed more than the land offered freely. I doubted that treasures such as glass would ever be found in the clean world, Juper or not. I knew that those which were pure had been destroyed. How could he put such importance to a dream? I wondered how many days he would search for it. Would he loath me if he knew what I knew of metals? A tinge of fear set itself in me. What could I do? I would have to tell them someday. Should I have spoke it already?

Kenter returned with empty hands and a heavy sigh. I drew the last section of Lethia's hair through the brush, then dropped my grip on the top strands of hair. They fell like heavy feathers onto her back.

"Don't fret it, Kenter. It will show itself soon enough. You'll see," said Lethia.

I offered the wind the loose strands from the brush and dropped it by its handle onto the flowers in the basket. Then I rose from my knees and brushed her dark break-away hairs from the front of my legs.

"Well," I said, smoothing her mane with my palm. "Shall we go?"

Lethia picked up our items and stood.

"Yeah," they said in unison.

We were now more than certain no one would come today.

"You know," said Lethia as we strode down the hill. "Rather than doing this twice a month, we could make a path for them to follow to the hillhouse, one that could not be easily moved by the weather. Perhaps I could design one of stones, or logs all in a row... now that you have working hands."

She had not thought it right. She was thinking on her need for architecture.

"Leth," said Kenter, "They could come through injured."

The memory of Kenter's entry to this world ran over Lethia's face like a dreaded wave.

"We should trade turns at it," I said interrupting her embarrassment. "We don't all need to share in the wait."

"We know how to keep safe now," said Kenter. "Only one need come."

"Two," I corrected him.

I was not confident Lethia could hold her own weight on this matter. She strongly feared beasts.

"One can stay at the hillhouse and garden. It's safer here with two," I explained.

"Nowhere here is truly safe from the beasts," said Lethia. "I do miss the protection of the pods."

Kenter changed the subject.

"I'm hungry," he said. "What should we eat tonight?"

"I'll cook cactus… if you take your turn and water the garden," I said playfully.

I turned to Lethia with a smile.

"We'll keep him out of the kitchen."

"I'll cook the cactus," he replied. "Yours is too crispy."

Lethia burst out a laugh.

"Oh, yes. Your cactus is superb," she cut in.

I laughed at their teasing. When Kenter tried to cook cactus, we, all three, ended up eating mostly berries for dinner in its stead. It took a whole day of boiling and soaking to scrape the pot clean. We all knew my cactus was best.

The breeze in the grasses painted the tops of our feet as we walked toward the hillhouse, each having food on our mind.

Chapter Twenty Two

It started to rain. The ground thirsted for it. Tolomay stepped out to the darkness and took in the air of it. The touch of its soft breath spun wonder in her heart. Daylight rain blocked the sun and made her tired, but night rain gave her bliss. Her skin drank in its cool pleasure.

The day was hot, and the moon had not yet cooled the air. Kenter followed her and shut the heavy door behind them, leaving Lethia to herself inside. Tolomay easily smelled the salt on his skin. She knew, without looking, he had stripped off his cover and wore only his bottom garb now.

The thought ran in tingles down the back of her neck, his warmth almost drawing her to touch him as he brushed past her, and then stood close. She fought against the yearning of her fingers, glad she could not see his chest and arms in the dark.

It became increasingly harder lately, not to stare at his naked chest and abdomen. He was so beautiful. Every muscle showed itself in a taut, defined manner. Until Kenter arrived, she had never seen a male's chest or thighs. Dress laws at the pod community had been strict. They forbade the showing of flesh between the bottom of the neck and the knees, except, of course, for forearms the hands. It kept citizens' thoughts at a comfortable distance, and staved off temptations of sharing reproductive pleasures, which protected females and infants against fatal physical birthings. Non-physical law pertained to all under twenty. At that point, eggs and sperm were gathered before mandatory sterilizations took place. Dress was different in the clean world. Flesh was not an issue here, and in this heat, Kenter and the two females were grateful for it.

"Your garden will smile in the morn," he said, his voice piercing the dark.

Tolomay turned his direction.

"I love the smell of the rain after it claims its place in the world," she answered. "The change in the feel of the air before it begins, and how the scent of the ground mingles with it to make a new one all its own, afterward."

Kenter loved the rain too and breathed it in deeply, but at present, he was thinking about Tolomay's skin, not the weather. For the first time in his life he realized how effective the pod medicines had been in squashing the desire of male's libidos. Tonight he was sure the medicine's effect had worn off completely.

There was not an ounce of Testrophine in his system and he was having difficulty holding back his desire. Mize's training of hormonal facts had in no way prepared him for this. Those humorous lessons at the pod were nothing like living his present shocking reality. Tolomay's distraction was nearly more than he could bear. His thoughts ran only to her flesh. She smelled of sweet oils. He could not seem to stifle his yearning.

"Tolomay," he said, touching her shoulder.

As softly as a breeze upon her, his fingers traced from her shoulder and down her wet arm. Stopping at her wrist, he set his hand underneath and slid his fingers up her palm until his hand was holding hers. She did not move. Her heart raced, feelings overwhelmed her.

She could not allow this, and as protector had an obligation to them all, she told herself. He did not yet know everything. But no matter her thoughts, she could no longer deny her emotions. They'd grown in strength each day. As she fought against herself, he caressed her other hand and his heat crept up her arm like a gentle flame. Her nervousness set goosebumps running down her body with the rain. She was afraid of this. She should stop it.

"Kenter," she said softly. "Don't…"

And then she saw it.

"Look at that!" she said, changing the subject.

"Don't look at what?" he replied, now caressing her other arm.

"No!" she shouted, abruptly jerking both arms away.

He was stunned. Had he thought it wrong? Did she feel it as well? Then he noticed her shadowed face viewing the trees.

"That!" she said pointing to the night.

Kenter turned. At a distance, near the tree line, a tiny green light glowed in the pitch black. It frolicked in the grasses, far away from the two, as if a giant green firefly.

"It's not a sunbug," he said.

"Firefly," she corrected him. "…and no, it is not. What is it? I've not seen it here before."

Kenter shot her his surprise.

"The Juper!" he shouted, and ran toward it.

"Wait!" she stopped his feet.

"Does a Juper move on its own accord?" she asked.

They watched its awkward movements.

"No," he said. "Not on its own."

Tolomay opened the door just a sliver.

"Lethia," she called into the house.

As Lethia stepped out, Kenter entered and returned moments later with a lit torch. He handed it to Tolomay, then went back inside.

"What's happened?" asked Lethia.

"That bear's got my Juper!" Kenter said, stepping outside with two more lit torches.

He pushed one toward Lethia.

Tolomay stopped the door from closing. She viewed Lethia's gentle eyes.

"Do you *want* to come?" she asked.

Lethia did not hesitate.

"Yes," she nodded. "I'll go."

They shut door and the three stepped toward the dancing green light in the distance.

"Do not get too near," Tolomay directed as they closed in on a growling sound. "Just wave the torches and scare him enough that he'll drop it. He will not fight against three torches."

"And don't surround him," commanded Kenter. "Leave him an escape."

"Yes," she agreed. "We must stay close together. Lethia, stay between us."

When the three neared the light, Lethia gripped her torch so tightly, she worried her fingers would embed in it for all eternity. She was terrified of that beast. But as they approached, they discovered it wasn't the bear at all.

Several shadowed beasts fought over the Juper. The size of large dogs, they pulled up their top lips to brag sharp teeth. One held the Juper in his mouth, as the others fought him for it. The bright green rod caused eerie fangs and brightly glowing nostrils. The creature abandoned it to the grasses at the notice of three humans, now, interested in only them.

The three found themselves surrounded as the beasts encircled them. With Kenter, Tolomay and Lethia back to back, each waved their flames to keep safe. There was no escaping the darkness.

"What are they?" asked Kenter, as the snarling grew nearer.

"Coyotes," answered Tolomay. "Or wolves. It is too dark to tell."

"Does it matter?" shouted Lethia. "Will they eat us?"

No one answered. Kenter looked at the glowing green stick, just a short distance away.

"No, Kenter." said Tolomay, in a frantic voice.

"I know," he answered.

He would never get to the Juper from where they stood trapped.

"They're closer!" squealed Lethia.

"I know!" he shouted, waving the torch to intimidate the beast, the creature so close the flame almost reached its face, it's eyes reflected in angry red.

Tolomay's torch began to flicker.

"The rain!" she shouted. "It's thinning the oils!"

Just as fast, her light went out and the pitch black engulfed her. Even as Kenter turned his light away from his own beast, he lost sight of her. There was growling and the sound of Tolomay's struggling.

"Tolomay!" he screamed to the darkness, frantically waving the flame to find her. "Tolomay!"

He could not see her, but they could hear her.

"Kenter!" Lethia called out in terror.

A yelp was heard, and then another. Then footsteps brought Tolomay into Lethia's light as she grabbed up the sister's torch, hand and all, and lit the area where her creature lay dead. Wet oozed from its head. Tolomay had killed it.

"Show them to me!" she shouted, out of breath as she wiped the rain from her brow. "My torch is a club! Protect your necks!"

No sooner had she spoken, a second beast charged, this time at Lethia. Tolomay batted it with her club, but missed its head entirely, striking only its shoulders. It fell to the ground, quickly recovered and lunged at her leg. Lethia kicked its hind end with the heel of her foot, and as it leapt to her, pressed the torch to its face. It yelped in agony and ran off. Kenter stepped toward the third. Gnashing its teeth, it aimed at his neck. Tolomay struck it mid-air. The beast landed on Kenter knocking both to the ground.

"Aaaaah!" he screamed as it clawed its dazed fury into his chest.

While its teeth struggle for his face, Tolomay held it by the scruff of its neck with all her might. No matter how strong it was, she would not let go. Her fingers burrowed into its thick coat so deeply that they almost touched her palm. Clenching tightly, she held its face up, as Lethia set the torch to its eye. The air smelled of burnt fur and made hissing sounds as the creature screamed. Tolomay released her grip and it ran off, yelping into the night.

The Juper began to move. Eight glowing eyes peered at them through the dark. There were more!

Lethia's torch began to flicker.

"The trees!" shouted Tolomay as she grabbed Lethia's dying torch and led the way.

Lethia and Tolomay were at their tree first. Kenter took another. Up, up, up they went, into the slimy wet of the pine bark. The needles were scratchy, but the first branches were low and close enough together that they climbed fast. Soon they were high above the ground, safe.

"You two all right?" he shouted to the rain.

"Yes," both females answered together.

"Your chest?" shouted Tolomay.

"Just a scratch," he answered.

The creatures lingered at the tree trunks for some time; then night fell to silence. Kenter watched as his Juper ran off and disappeared into the distant woods, taking his life's purpose and his dream of metals with it.

~ ~ ~

When day tiptoed in with drier feet, the three viewed Tolomay's dead beast in the grasses below. They saw it clearly now.

"They were wolves," she said, as she climbed down. "They must have been hungry, or they would not have attacked."

"The Juper is living energy," replied Kenter. "They must have viewed it as food."

"Perhaps," said Tolomay. "But they will only attack humans if they are starving."

"Why did they not eat the dead wolf then?" he asked, jumping to the ground.

"A wolf is not a cannibal, Kenter. They can be more loyal to one another, than some humans have been in the past. A wolf will even raise a human infant as its own. They are allies to humanity and are most kind creatures. Only the ones across seas in ancient Eurmany, were murderous."

Kenter inspected his wounds. Stepping to the ground, Lethia wriggled her feet into the wet grasses and stared at her brother's injuries.

"Kind. Hmm," she said under her breath.

She was still shaken, even after the hours that had unfolded. Tolomay stepped them to the lifeless wolf.

"The poor thing was hungry," she said as she knelt petting its grey coat. "Even at that he has offered *us* food, now. His fur will be warm, and we can use his precious fat to make oil we've been short of. His death will not have gone to waste, as no creature's death ever should.

"Two lessons of wolves... you can tell one at a distance. It will not raise its tail up higher than its hind end, as a dog does…and never eat a wolf's innards. The knowledge of which inside parts are edible, was lost long ago. Some can be poisonous and will kill us. But those can still be used for tanning. I will show you which of his organs are best for it. Still, his muscles and fats can be eaten and put to use. This one has much meat. If we dry it, we can eat for weeks without hunting."

Tolomay removed the thick strapping from her waist. She tied it as a pull rope to the beast's front legs. By the time they dragged it home, they were exhausted and hungry.

~ ~ ~

After Tolomay scrubbed Kenter's wounds clean, his chest bled four red lines. They began at his shoulder and ran at a strange angle across his rib cage. They were superficial injuries, but once again she and Lethia would have to patch him. His perfect chest would be marked for a while. The females stepped to the kitchen to prepare the wound sap paste.

Lethia had not spoken this morning. Though very fit and physically strong, her trauma from last night's desperate battle seemed evident. She had never been so close to a beast, not even the great bear. Tolomay tried to lighten the mood while they ground at the herbs with course stones.

"You know there will be no peace here now," she teased sarcastically. "We are in the presence of the survivor of a fierce wolf attack."

Lethia's fingers stopped grinding. She was at the verge of tears.

"Lethia."

"Yes," Lethia whispered.

"You were brave last night," said Tolomay, pulling her into a hug. "Thank you."

After a moment, she pushed her head back enough to meet Lethia's eyes.

"It was good you came with us," Tolomay continued. "Kenter and I may not be alive if you had not. You likely saved us all Lethia, you and your powerful legs, and your burning torch. You are stronger than you know…even with the beasts."

A tear ran down Lethia's cheek.

"I'm just very glad we're all safe from them. I did not think it I would fear them so much. I miss the safety of home," she answered softly.

Tolomay nodded understanding. Her heart felt concern as the two turned to finish the paste. It was not due to the beasts.

Chapter Twenty Three

The small wooden spoon twirled easily in his hand, as Kenter licked its heel for the last taste of wolf soup. Tolomay lay on her bedding, a small piece of gray fur in her hand.

"The warm mixture preserves the pelts, though I barely have the heart to do it at times. But it is the most effective way to tan hides, so their offering of skins and furs do not stiffen, or rot and go to waste."

Lethia sat holding Carmella. As much as she did not like fierce beasts, she understood Tolomay's feelings regarding the use of the animal's own brains to preserve its pelt. It seemed barbaric.

She kissed Carmella's head. She had grown attached to this pet and was glad Tolomay had thought to feed her, to entice her to stay upon arrival here. Pets were forbidden at the pods. It was considered a risk of disease and a waste of nourishing foods to keep the mice as mere toys for children, though as they all knew, every child dreamed of keeping a pet.

"I tire of not having metal forks," said Kenter, examining the medieval style wooden utensil.

"Stop yourself, Kenter. Again…you cannot think it…" Tolomay answered. "…things of the community."

There was a long pause before she continued.

"It will divide your heart," she explained.

"Yeah..." answered Kenter sarcastically. He laid the spoon atop the side of the bowl, holding one finger from each hand beneath it, to keep it in place. "I greatly miss re-store duty," he finished sarcastically.

He attempted to balance the spoon on the bowls edge, but coordination evaded him. It kept slipping to one side and finally fell to the table.

Tolomay smiled. She knew what he referred to. Everyone hated re-store duty. It entailed collecting items for compost from the kitchen bins each night. The smell was unbearable. What was not composted was fed to the crabs. Everyone had duty of sorting leftovers, when their turn was scheduled. Even though it a torturous task, not even the elders were immune, though they were usually the ones rewarded with the precious meats from the crabs.

"Don't hear him, Tolomay. Most times someone else did his, usually Arden."

Kenter's face drew into his thoughts. Tolomay knew this feeling. He showed it for only a fleeting moment before he swept it away, but not in time to hide it from the females.

"Sorry, brother," said Lethia. "I know he was your truest friend."

He watched as Lethia's eyes returned to the creature in her lap. Kenter knew she had many more friends than he, and she missed them as well.

"There are things that will pass through your memory," Tolomay said. "But we can never go back. Training does not prepare for the longing of the heart when the clean world is thrust upon us, no matter how glorious and breathtaking it is. Nothing is the same, but we cannot carry the past into this world. We must go forward. They sent us forward."

Neither twin replied. Tolomay could see it, the plague of homesickness. It was slowly, yet sporadically becoming a shadow, more so from Lethia than Kenter. Still, if not stifled soon, it could breed itself into something enormous. She knew first hand. This had not been the only notice she'd had of it, nor the only conversation about the pods that lingered in the air between them recently. She needed to take action.

She remembered her grief upon arriving here alone, and although the twins had each other and her to rely upon, they were feeling despairs each their own. Missing the pod community did not fill the spirit as living for the day, and stagnation rested at its door.

Tolomay did not want to return to the site, but thought it best if they had a change of space for a day or two. Perhaps it was time they knew the rest of it. After all, it would eventually come. She would have to take them there. Sooner would likely be better than later, she reasoned, and Kenter was healed. He was more than well enough for the trip. With their recent shows of nostalgia, it seemed a logical decision.

Tolomay's heavy sigh, and her silence afterward, drew Lethia's attention away from the lizard.

"When I first came through," Tolomay began, "I had no set place to lay myself down at night. Tarron told me do not wander from this place, so I did not.

"I slept by the tree line the first few nights, listening to dark sounds, my mind choked with fear. I felt as if I were waiting in a painful dream.

"Though, for what I cannot tell you, because I do not know, perhaps for my heart to catch up with me. My legs were idle and I did not care. I was ill prepared to do even the smallest things, despite the fact I had trained extensively for them.

"More than any of the others, I was trained to survive. They knew what might happen before they sent us, that we might not all make it. I believe they knew. I think even Tarron knew, though he did not tell me. But I was trained for it, survival on my own."

She sat up to tell the rest.

"Being in this great space alone was

more than I could bear, so I was unable to use the training I knew so well. My thoughts were flooded with sights, and sounds, and smells, that so filled me, at moments I thought I would burst.

"But I was alone and could think to nothing of what tasks I must do to stay alive in this enormous world. I was tired from no rest, though my body did not work. Then I became weak. Whilst I lay upon the hill watching a butterfly spin its wings to the sky, I made a decision to leave this place.

"My thoughts took my feet to land that is far from here. I marked my path so I would not get lost if ever I decided to return. I searched for herbs and berries to eat so I would not starve without hunting, following the edible trail as I stepped my feet."

Lethia listened intently, so much so that she did not watch as Carmella slid from her hand. Tolomay did, and viewed the lizard skitter across the floor as she continued.

"At first I did not think it I could kill a beast, even to eat. But I knew the herbs by sight and shape, and many by taste, but not all. Most of the ones in our garden I had never seen live or held before coming here. So I wandered for a day and filled my stomach with them. Then I came to a place. I want you to see it."

Kenter's heart always ached when Tolomay talked this way. It was as if a trance took her for a time, and then would return her when it was finished. He would never go through what she had, and would never feel such compassion for another because of it. The thought she was a mere thirteen years old at the time, made it all that much more tragic to his ears.

"A place?" Lethia asked.

"Kenter," Tolomay said. "Do not allow yourself anger toward me when at first you see it."

Lethia and Kenter's eyes met. He could not believe that after what she had just shared, she'd be worried about his anger. He could not imagine how a place could make him angry with Tolomay.

"What is this place?" he asked.

"You will see," was the most she would offer the two. "It is a day's walk, so we will need to pack enough to stay the eve. Let's rest early tonight and awake with the sun."

Tolomay did not mentioned the place before, because she thought she knew what Kenter would think if she did. He would want to take things from there. After last night, he'd likely be furious, but because of the recent talk of the community these past few days, she felt they needed it as much as she had the day she'd found it. She drifted to her thoughts again.

"Tolomay, I'll take a torch for if the wolves come," Kenter said smartly.

"Then I'd best bring some wound sap," she replied snidely, teasing about his uselessness that night.

She was back. He could see it in the exasperated roll of her eyes. Once again, he'd brought her back within his reach.

Lethia picked up Carmella.

"Carmella cannot come," said Tolomay. "She will get lost."

"She needs a wed match, Tolomay" replied Lethia, "A male, to keep her company when we go away."

She was thinking of taking a pet of her own, as she kissed the lizard's head.

Tolomay smiled and smoothed the flat blanket to lay down. Tomorrow might be difficult, the least of it being the letter.   She had not yet disclosed everything. Her eyes fell to Kenter as he spread out his bedding.   What if after their journey, nothing was the same?

Chapter Twenty Four

They'd been walking half the day. Kenter watched Tolomay laugh her hysteria so fiercely, she held her stomach in an attempt to keep it from aching. Joy of life danced in her eyes as she stopped her feet in the middle of the grasses.

He knew being alone here had dimmed pieces of her heart. That's why he loved to make her happy, to help refill what had been taken from her, or at least as best he could.

"And he believed you?" she asked, still laughing.

He just smiled.

"Kenter, you're evil. Who would believe one could backstroke in the Pool of Light?"

"Well, the child he told the tale to, was only six," said Lethia.

That made Tolomay laugh all that much harder. This time she fell to the ground. Kenter's wide smile turned to the sound of a chuckle.

"Oooh," said Tolomay, as she lay upon the soft grass, "My stomach hurts, shall we stop here and rest?"

"I'm hungry," he exclaimed, dropping down beside her.

"So am I," said Lethia.

They found the offering of shade from a great tree nearby.

"This is an elm," Tolomay remarked as the others studied its trunk and then viewed its strange and crooked reach. "See its bark? And the leaves? Look how great and old this one is."

She made an exerted effort, recently, to teach things of this world in passing conversation, rather than leading them from place to place as she'd done when they'd arrived. Her original method of teaching bothered Kenter, but she'd known no other and so mimicked Tarron's ways. She remembered from infancy, while still in her bedlet, her father's constant trainings. Tarron had led her from book to book, thing to thing, place to place, within the community grounds and labs, teaching her most minutes of her existence. She knew of little else than learning. Her education had been like breath to her lungs, and she held it close to her core, as if it were the most treasured gift of time itself.

Lethia spread her blanket upside down on the ground for the others to share. Tolomay removed a bundle of skins from her bag. She un-wrapped the articles of food they packed this morning, and laid them upon the skin. Her eyes were drawn to the landscape. They were half way there.

Kenter spoke through a mouthful of berries.

"So if you left a trail the first time, and it's been three years, then how do you know where you're leading us?" he asked, sarcastically. "How do we *know* you can find us our way back there?"

Lethia looked to her brother. He knew Tolomay's memory would not forget such a thing. He was being foolish, and only asked to get her response, but Tolomay complied.

"I set it in my mind to pay attention to my path upon my return to the hill," she answered. "I knew that if others came, there would be a time I would want to share what I saw on my travels."

Lethia sat eating, curious as to where

they were going. She was excited about the adventure and could no longer hold the question in her mind.

"Is it a grand place, Tolomay? Like a waterfall? Or a cavern?" she asked.

Tolomay answered with a serious tone.

"It's not that kind of beautiful place, Lethia, but not all caverns are grand, truly. Some are musty and filled with molds and bacterium that can lead to great illnesses. Some contain deadly creatures or ones that carry disease. You should always use caution when you..."

At the look of Lethia's worried eyes, she realized the impact of her words.

"We will be safe from beasts, Lethia. Worry not...and we are not going to a cavern. But there is amazement in our path to the place," she remarked, forcing a smile. "You will not believe what you see at one spot of beautiful earth on the way."

This was a hard trip for Tolomay. Grateful for Kenter's jokes, she tried not to think of their destination, for now. It brought memories, feelings she'd otherwise choose to forget. She wanted to revisit them only once, only while there and was growing more and more fearful of Kenter's reaction to the place. Would he forgive her? Would he view her with different eyes after today?

"So what made you so determined to swim, anyway, Kenter?" Tolomay asked, changing the subject that haunted her mind.

The truth sounded ridiculous. He didn't want to speak it, his feeling of needing to be in the clean world, as if he was meant to go, his dreams and thoughts of being first in this place nearly since birth, the desire for it so strong it almost held a taste. Pondering the clean world brought heat into his heart. It was a heat he had yearned for and one he'd felt wholeheartedly each day since he and Lethia arrived. But how could he tell her that? Kenter glanced to his sister.

"I couldn't let her go alone," he said. "What if she came through injured?"

Kenter's lips curled to a smile, while the females glanced at one another. Tolomay rolled her eyes.

"Grasp it, Kenter, that pun's once old," said Lethia, then she poked his side with her finger.

Her brother was trying very hard to keep Tolomay's attention, and it was a pleasure for her to watch his efforts. For once, a female was not chasing behind *him*.

After their bellies were full, they rested for a session and then continued on their way. A short while later, the landscape changed with each step of their feet. Plant life began to diminish to spatters of green splotches here and there until, like a line drawn onto the Earth, the grasses disappeared all at once.

In their place, dirt and stone emerged, but it did not look like the dirt in the garden. For a time nothing green lay upon the ground, not a tree, nor bush, nor a blade of grass. The rock seemed out of place, like one that did not belong on this pure clean Earth, from a different world entirely.

The twins watched as the color of the stone grew blacker as they walked. This didn't appear as indigenous rock, not ones of mountains they'd studied in training. Instead, it seemed to have been melted from the inside out, and then reformed in an ugly manner.

It stunk with the breath of something unthinkable, the stench nearly unbearable, worse than meat left to rot in the heat of the summer. They were each three silent, for the longest time. The place left holes in their hearts. Something had happened here, something horrific, something devastating, something they surely did not want to know about. This Earth was dead. It felt ruined, like a soul shattered to a million pieces. They walked for miles without speaking a word, until Kenter broke the silence.

"Nothing will live here again," he said.

The females did not need to answer. They felt the surety of his truth. Step by step they continued onward until soon enough, trees and leaves and plants began pouring their color once again onto the Earth before them. They walked through a long forest, which turned so dark to their eyes it seemed almost night, until bit by bit the sun began bursting in lines through the thinning trees and they came near a clearing in its wake.

Tolomay turned to watch their faces. She wanted to see their expressions as they entered this place. The twin's eyes widened as they stepped through the trees into perfection. Their smiles grew, pushing their cheeks up in amazement.

"It's beautiful," said Lethia, in awe of the sight.

Rows and rows of lump-like bushes had been planted in display as trees once were in the manicured yards of the ancients. They were perfectly aligned and the view seemed endless, as if to extend the whole of the Earth. Though ivy had woven its way between and around them, it was obvious there were thousands and thousands of these bumps laid out separately, yet in perfect unison. Tolomay was right. This was a magnificent sight.

"Take care not to trip," said Tolomay. "The vines like to grab at feet."

"What are they?" asked Kenter pressing on the waist high bundle of ivy, only to find a solid object was hidden beneath.

Lethia looked down at one nearest her feet. A small gray corner showed itself as a clue. She pushed it forward with her hide covered foot, before her face took on a sudden look of understanding.

"Graves," she said. "This one is of marble."

Kenter watched Tolomay to see if his sister was correct. She nodded.

"This is the yard where they buried their dead?" he asked.

"I studied of this," said Lethia. "They built houses made of wood and metal for each body and named them each the same surname of...Casket," she remembered.

Kenter interrupted before Tolomay could speak.

"Metals?" he asked.

He was hungry for them and Tolomay's heart grew suddenly unnerved. Dread seeded itself in the pit of her stomach. She ignored her sudden surge of adrenaline at his comment, and nodded to Lethia.

"This is just one of thousands upon thousands of places like this," she answered. "Trees have gotten most of them by now; but not as much in this one, I think it. The ivy here chokes even itself."

Kenter seemed shocked.

"The land in just one place like this would have housed and farmed a hundred communities. Instead, they used them to store their bones?"

Tolomay answered his unspoken question. "Some believed they could not move past death, without graves, that if they did not have them they would be stuck in the Earth forever," she said. "They were afraid, so they buried the bones."

"All this land," replied Kenter, with obvious disgust.

"I think they're beautiful," said Lethia as she led them through and around the planted stones. "Each one remembered and now covered in life of green. Besides, they believed their bodies would rise again. It was customary, Kenter. They held end of life celebrations, much like the Light Embracements at the pods. They called them *wakes*."

Tolomay's lips crawled up to a smile. She was glad Lethia was studied.

"We will dig up their metals," Kenter said, in a determined tone.

"Not today. They are buried deeper than we are tall," answered Tolomay. "It would take weeks."

"So?" he replied.

Tolomay let out an exasperated breath, now not only scared, but annoyed.

"Another time, Kenter, when Carmella is not locked in a cage."

Tolomay had come only for vines. It took nearly an hour for them to break loose enough stems from the growth as they needed. Kenter was quiet while he worked. When he uncovered one stone completely, all three bent closer for a better look at its engraved front.

"Look at the date," he said, stooping closer.

Tolomay leaned in and read aloud.

"It's written in Old American English. They used it before Merican. See the similarities?" she said pointing to the letters. "Sutton Brady, loving husband and father, 2089-2109."

"He was our age," said Kenter. "And now encased in what I need."

"He died five hundred years before I was born," added Tolomay, ignoring his comment. "Almost to the year. There was a great plague at that time, one of mass poisonings, deliberate poisonings of foods, but they guised it as a plague."

"We will come back, and dig these up. Did you know, Tolomay? About the metal cask..."

"Aaaaaah!" Lethia's scream cut the air in two.

Chills shot down Tolomay's back. She scanned their perimeter for a beast nearby, thinking Lethia had view of one. Seeing nothing awry, she threw eyes to Lethia. The twin, whining in agony, held up her forearm for them to see.

"Ah, ah, ah, get it off! Get it off! It bit, and left its teeth in me," she wailed. "It's fierce pain!"

Tolomay viewed the object that sat atop Lethia's arm. The venom sac was still intact. Kenter leaned in to see.

"It's a small, white clover flower," he said. "How can it bite?"

Tolomay pulled it from Lethia's skin and threw it to the grasses.

"It's a yellow jacket sac," said Tolomay. "...the inside of a bee. You must have brushed the rest away when it stung you."

Lethia's eyes teared instantly; a look of tragedy swept her face. She turned to Kenter with grave devastation.

"I will die now," she said.

Hysteria followed. Trembling with all her being, the sibling threw herself into her brother's arms.

Kenter was suddenly frantic, but surprise found Tolomay's face. She gently separated the twins and cupped her hand over the wound in a manner so as not to hurt Lethia, but rather to draw her attention.

"No, Lethia," said Tolomay, sincerity filling her eyes. "It is merely a bee sting. It will hurt all day, but you will be fine. No concerns. You will not die from this."

"Bees kill," Lethia argued, her heart petrified. "I *trained* in it. They kill. Their poisons are toxic. People are allergic."

Tolomay breathed out a breath. She did not want to diminish Lethia, but the number of people allergic to bees was of the lowest percentage.

"Almost none are," said Tolomay. "I am not. You will not be, either. You will be fine."

"Are you sure?" Kenter asked, watching the red welt grow upon his sister's arm. "You have been bit?"

"It's stung, not bit," Tolomay replied gently. "And yes. I've been stung a number of times."

Kenter worried as he watched the center of the spot swell to a tip. He pushed his face nearer, to examine it. His closeness to Tolomay made her uncomfortable. With his heat rolling her direction, her heart raced as the wings of a hummingbird. It excited her as she looked to him, but he hadn't even noticed. Instead, he inspected Lethia's red bump, touching it with his finger tip.

"Does it still hurt?" he asked.

Lethia pulled her arm away.

"Yes!" she replied, exasperated. "Leave it!"

"Go find whistle weed, Kenter," Tolomay told him. "We just passed some in the trees. Do you remember its view?"

Mize Maxy had drilled whistle weed into his memory so heavily that, though he had not viewed it close up until today, he knew its look quite well.

"I saw it hanging there, too," he said and trod back to the forest.

"Do not get lost!" shouted Lethia.

Tolomay inspected the wound before both females sat, leaning against the ivy covered head stones. Tolomay swatted the mosquito that landed on her arm.

"This is a great green kingdom and we sit at the thrones," Lethia teased, her eyes now absent of worry.

Tolomay smiled as they waited for Kenter in the graveyard, where the ancients had buried their dead.

M.E. Lorde

Tolomay's World and The Pool of Light

ChapTer Twenty Five

My nerves were easily as frayed as the ivy we stripped, the leaves settling into piles upon the ground. I'd left whatever small peace of mind I'd had about today's trip, back at the other side of this land with the mosquitoes and the bones in the ground. We were close now. The thought of it seeped in slowly, devouring my heart as we sat upon the grasses making ropes. I was far from being brave as I had been trained to be.

"Lethia, if you could grab a few more this length, I think it that will do wonderfully," I told her.

"Twist these ones, Kenter, please," I said in my kindest voice.

He was already angry about the caskets. Would he loathe me in a few hours time? I handed him an armful of vines. He said nothing as he took them. I was too polite this afternoon; but could not think it how to speak or move to hide what I was feeling.

I wondered if he felt the dread in my belly when he viewed my eyes. Would he still share his warmth with me after today? My weight grew heavier in my chest. All at once, I did not want to go. The closer we were, the more my burden grew. Where had my thought been in making this decision? What was best for the community, I decided. For the three of us, I could bear anything. But could I bear my most desolate moment of despair without tears showing themselves? I needed to.

Kenter had never seen me cry. Not really. The closest I'd come to shedding tears in his presence was the news of Tarron's death, but even then I had not cried before his eyes. Upon my return home that day, he had been asleep. He was used to viewing my anger by now, but if he saw how truly weak I was, would it change the way he looked upon me?

I did not want his view of me to see a timid, frail thing and there was very little I despised more than the feeling in my chest when tears flowed like a river down my cheeks. That was why I rarely allowed them. They always made my stomach ill afterward and forced the feeling of helplessness to take its grip upon my spirit. Had I not cried sufficiently when I'd lived it? There were no tears left for the time I spent in that place. It was in the past.

I had two great worries today, the affect of the place on both Kenter and me, and what the frame held. I closed my eyes and listened to the silence of the trees. It calmed my unsettled spirit, but only briefly.

"How much further?" he asked, interrupting my peace.

"A handful of miles. Five kilometers, perhaps ten, but likely five," I answered. "This won't take long, with us working together. The ropes to bind the smoke house walls took weeks."

"Are you certain these ones will hold?" he teased, referring to the state of the smokehouse from the bear's fury.

"I'm certain." I said, almost daring him to continue with his nonsense.

I was no longer in the mood for jokes or sarcasm and almost blamed him in some way... for the inevitable. So I just stared at him, my mouth turned up at the corners of my tensed lips. It was difficult enough for me to make this journey. I did not want the appeal that his presence forced into my heart when he stood so close, at least until this trip was finished, and if and when I decided to tell him everything. Perhaps that one detail could remain my secret for a while. I could not make up my mind.

It was an hour or so away, and I still had not decided how to tell him. I had to think it, since a lot depended on whether or not he would listen when we first arrived. We did not need an argument in that place unless it was a constructive one. Ours rarely were.

What would he do when we entered? I had warned him, but felt he would still be angry. Would he forgive me my secrets? Hardly. Would my heart keep me from thinking clearly? Perhaps.

The closer we got, the more I felt like a five-year-old child who did not want to choose a task. Trusting nothing in my thoughts as we sat in these grasses, I could not ignore my dismay. Today would upset the balance our community held; I realized it as fact while I sat pulling leaves. But not to go there would leave things unsaid that should not be. The twins needed to focus solely on our future here and after today, they would. I felt as a dizzy idiot, and it grew fiercer by the moment. I could not put reason to my thoughts.

The sun shone upon my shoulders. I closed my eyes to let its light take me for a moment. I was glad for it, but torn even in that. My heart raced a nervous race. If it rained this morning, I would not have brought them today. It was risky enough to be there when dry. At this moment, I preferred it had rained.

Would I have the courage to open what had been, and what might be, all in the same day? Fear pounded itself through me. I could not stop its flow. Even as it fell into my still feet, I heard each pound of my chest.

Lethia braided tightly, and was fast. Between the three of us, it wouldn't take much longer to complete the rope. I had better decide what to do. Her thoughts searched my quiet, though she said nothing. I could not think what to speak to fill the space between us.

As Kenter twisted the vines into long strands, I tried to distract my anxious breathing with observations. He had muscular arms for his height. So did Lethia. I imagined the Vision Fold had required them more physical exercise than when I was a candidate; after all, my group's training was more intellectually based, even in our survival training.

None in my group had been athletes, but the twins, obviously were. Though Lethia was physically strong, her heart was still untarnished and tender. Real strength comes from a place deeper than arms and legs that she had not yet found. She did not know how truly strong she could be. I had learned the hard way and without choice. It had been forced upon me, just as the responsibility of this trip. My feet whispered their tingles to my shoes.

The grasses' wondrous scent rose into the still air. I loved its sweet embrace and wanted to keep this moment in my mind for the rest of the journey, to keep thoughts away from the place. But the feeling passed almost as swiftly as it came, and I could not hold its company before a breeze blew it away.

Kenter sat down beside me with more strands between his fingers. He fastened their ends to the others for Lethia and I to braid into the rest. The rope danced and swung as he pulled the knots taught. It would hold.

I could not avoid the closeness of his shoulders and arms nor could I draw myself from this abyss of past pain. It cast its heavy shadow over my mind. I stood in an effort to escape them both and walked from the twins, into the woods. I could think not one thought correctly. Not one. I needed time alone.

A log offered itself for me to rest upon the pines. I had to logic it out, plan it right. What was I doing?

Tarron had warned against making rash decisions based on impulse. I feared this was what he meant. Perhaps I thought it wrong to come back here at all. Still, in spite of my current emotions, I had to be logical. It was too late to turn back around. We were almost there. The tingling of my toes held the eyes of the rest of me.

There were two ways the stream could flow today. Kenter would either think me weak, or we would argue. I had to be the stronger of us both, no matter all else. He could not view me as weak. The issue at hand was the effect he had on me, warming me as the sun, muddling my mind like a hive full of bees. It caused a stir within me, a feeling of falling and flying all at once. All logic seemed to dissolve when it came. In many ways it left me helpless.

Tarron told me to keep close to the males who drew my happiest thoughts. Despite our arguments, I'd never known one more suited than Kenter. Though presently the only male here, I knew regardless of how many others arrived in this place, he would always be my choice. Having the traits I would have searched for in a match, even in his arrogance, he held a fierce loyalty that could not be ignored. That was the trait I would count on today. I feared it would abandon me.

Tarron also told me to separate emotion from logic. Aside from my first week here, and until I met Kenter, there had been no easier task. But it was not easy today. I did not want to know what would happen once we arrived. What would he think? How would he react? I was so scared.

If he pitied me, it would make all things harder in the future. I was terrified I would fold in two and allow him to carry my weight. I felt he would. I could not do it. The responsibility had been laid upon my shoulders, not his.

If he did not believe it, would he fight against my lead? Worse yet, what if he did believe? Either way, I would lose him, but I would lose my mind if I did not move past this fear. Tarron would scold me for it if he were here. Where was my logic? I would have to close my heart this day, to keep my emotions away.

I did not have the strength to tell it all, I decided. Not today. He could know my secret a different time. They did not need it all at once. It would change our days.

That was logical, right, Tarron? Basic information of the letter and then information about my homesickness was enough for their hearts to hear today, and more than enough for mine. If Kenter would listen at the beginning, he would understand later when I finish. Lethia will be easier. She is a great listener. He is hot headed.

Lethia stepped into the woods. When she saw me sitting, she motioned for Kenter.

Both stared at the trees behind me,

their eyes wild with joy. I turned to view what they saw. At a distance, a large creature stood on four legs. It was broad shouldered and sleek, with mighty horns upon its head, its thin snout held high. We watched quietly as it stood proudly silent, smelling at the air with its glorious face. It was a beastly angel and my heart overflowed with utter peace. It flicked its ears, then suddenly, like lightening, leapt gracefully through the brush and into the thick woods. I had been so deep in despair I hadn't even heard it's hooves on the leafy carpet behind me.

"Moose, right?" asked Lethia.

"Close… a stag… the family is deer," I said, then stood. "The female's heads do not brag the massive antlers. Their name is doe."

Lethia smiled, her eyes glistening even in the shadows. I felt stronger now. I could do this task. The creature lent me his strength.

"Our rope is finished," Lethia said.

"Good. We must gather small sticks and bring them and the ivy leaves. We will line our extra shoe skins with them once we arrive at the place."

"Why?" Kenter asked.

"To thicken their bottoms and keep injury from our feet," I answered, bluntly.

I ignored Kenter and Lethia's questioning glances as we headed back to the grasses and rope. I had no energy left for courtesy today. My task was at hand.

Tolomay's World and The Pool of Light

Chapter Twenty Six

"Touch nothing before you in this place," Tolomay's words held a seriousness that was not to be overlooked.

A thick row of tall bushes grew up like a high wall before them, preventing them from seeing what was beyond. She pointed at their thorns.

"Take care," she directed, and they stretched their necks closer, so to view the threat.

Using broken branches, Tolomay swept the vines aside to disclose the sight.

Lethia let out a gasp. The twins could not believe their eyes. The three took turns holding the sticks, so the one behind could walk through without getting stuck, and then they stood together. This was it, the place Tolomay had spoken of, but had not explained.

Lethia's face lit up, but Kenter simply raised his chin and clenched his jaw as he stared in disbelief.

It was as if a land of treasures had opened up before them, but was in ruins at the same time. All things of the past sat crumbled, with pieces of yesterday's useful items stuck into the dirt and grasses and weeds that had grown up on the mountains of it. Piles of rubbish had become piles of treasures as one time moved into the next. Here, were much needed items that would greatly ease their burdens and help with living in this clean world.

Old box computers, metal objects and pieces of damaged electronics seemed salvageable for parts. Appliances, great and small lay buried in the ground and the green of plant life, in its small sprigs, had just begun to claim its settlement in the rubble. Some things were half disintegrated and rusty and falling apart, some were melted together and ruined and in pieces, but enough was there that the twins could see these bits of gems could be invaluable to them.

Most of what lay before them was light grey dirt, but so many objects poked their head up to peer at them, they could imagine what treasures must lay beneath the miles long piles of gray. Pieces of stone, as if from buildings, were heaped over several areas of the land. A marble path that seemed less disturbed was covered with broken bits of glass and roofing and automobiles that lay on their backs, with vines and trees and grasses growing from their bellies. Yesterday's glory lay painted before them on the canvas of its demise. It was the greatest buried treasure of all time, and all of it at their disposal.

Tolomay drew Kenter's eyes away with a stare. She knew what he was thinking, of metals and electronic treasures, and her eyes told him no. She had directed against it, so he would oblige, for now. And she'd been correct when she warned him yesterday. She'd said '*Do not allow yourself anger with me when you see it,*' yet he had.

He was very furious, but said nothing. Why had she not told him of her great secrets? He wanted these items. They would change everything for him, for them. They risked themselves in their attempt to retrieve the Juper from the wolves, all three had, risked their very lives, yet she said nothing about the metal caskets, or the metals buried here.

His heart instantly soaked up the stain of betrayal, like a dry cloth, dropped into a stream. How could she have kept all this from him? He would never forgive her. Any one of them could have died, and for nothing. It suddenly dawned on him that she was not loving. She was selfish. Did she care nothing at all for him? These were metals! Everywhere he looked! He tucked his fury into his stomach, for now. He wanted to see more.

Tolomay pointed to the other side of the canvas. The ground had exploded from the inside out and left bits of metal and stone melded together there. The structure rose a hundred feet into the air like a tower, but not one that had been built. It was made from a blast that had spewed itself out, from deep within the Earth.

The structure was shear and the sky shown through it, with the look of the skin of a snake when done with its youth and has left it behind in the grasses. The ground and stone at the base were rippled and melted. Large protrusions spit out from its bottom, curling up to shapes that resembled fingers. It looked like Earth was the hand, and it held in its palm, the eerie evidence for all to see, the destruction of men of the past.

Tolomay kept walking. Lethia and Kenter followed, as she led them to an area with less debris. They approached what seemed a round marble fountain about waste high, or so the twins thought. A piece of board leaned against it. As Kenter and Lethia approached, Tolomay set her hand upon a rounded board that seemed nearly petrified, as if almost stone, but not quite. It was half the size of the top of the fountain. What should have been a circle was shaped like an arch, with one side broken crookedly down what would have been its center.

"This is what I sat upon," she said. "Well, half of what I sat upon," she corrected herself.

She patted at it and the heavy board rolled on its round edge until it met the broken section, and then fell, wobbling its strange dance until it lay flat upon the ground.

Lethia didn't understand any of this. Tolomay's eyes wore sadness, and her face looked drawn since they'd left the graveyard. Why had she kept this place secret? Something weighed heavily on her, and she was talking in riddles. It was as if she didn't want to be here, as if she didn't want to tell them something. If that was the case, then why did she bring them, and why could they not look for useful items to take back home, since the ground had saved them in its bosom?

"Where's the other half?" asked Kenter, coldly.

He wanted information. Tolomay turned to the fountain and pointed to its center.

"Down there," she said.

Kenter and Lethia stepped to the edge of the marble lined well. They peered inside. It was twenty or so feet deep and no water rested at its bottom, but rather it bragged a marble floor. The sides were slightly tilted, but barely. With the sun shining on its white insides, the bottom could easily be seen from where they stood at the top. Inside lay the missing piece of Tolomay's round board; beside it, a large slate-like box. On top of it, something shone in the sunlight. It appeared as glass, but Kenter could not make out what it was from this angle.

Whatever it was, he wanted it. She'd kept glass from him as well? He stared at her.

"So, you were sitting here," he said, wondering what was going on in her selfishly secretive head. "Is that it? And you fell in?"

Tolomay nodded in agreement. He was growing tired of this game.

"Can you not just *answer* the question?" he asked as if she meant nothing to him.

She'd been correct. This trip had changed everything already and he had not even heard the end of it.

"Hand me the rope," she replied slowly, her heart drenched in sorrow. "I will show you."

Kenter and Lethia caught each other's gaze before they helped Tolomay tie the vine rope securely to a large chunk of bent up road at the side of the well. It was enormous and heavy and would not move, so the three had no worries of their return to the top.

Tolomay was the last one down, grief filling her as she climbed. She felt ill as her feet touched the floor. Lethia touched at the sides of the smooth marble wall, while Kenter admired the letter which lay on display in a clear plastic encasement, two inches thick. The slate box supported it and framed the letter. He stared at the paper. It was illegible to him.

He viewed the floor where lay a dark stain. Another, the same color, hung on the wall beside him; only the one on the wall held the mark of a handprint, much smaller than his hand would leave. He set his palm across it to compare its small fingers with his then mentally compared the size of Tolomay's hand. Similar prints ran up the wall, but none so clear as this one. The weather and sunlight had faded the others.

Lethia stood beside her brother. She could not fathom how this open place kept from filling with water until she saw the rectangular drainage holes around its edges. They were nearly hidden. The bottom of the well was somehow hollow. It smelled dank.

Kenter turned back to the letter.

"What language?" he asked while inspecting it further. "Do you know?"

"Yes," remarked Tolomay. "I know it. Watch," she said urging him to one side.

Once they switched places, she tapped at a small rectangular tile that lay directly in front of the box. Unless they knew to look, they might have missed it altogether, but she knew it was there. Suddenly, the frame's encasement dropped into the stone and disappeared. She tapped her foot and it rose again for all to see.

The twins smiled at one another. It was similar to the equipment back home. Kenter knew pieces from this device would prove invaluable to them. He would find a way to take it apart once Tolomay explained why she had brought them. He tried hard to conceal his impatience for her to be finished, so he could take what he needed.

"What does it say?" he asked.

Tolomay didn't need to see it to read. She remembered it verbatim. She would, in all certainty, have remembered it even without her great memory. She had read it enough times; so while Lethia continued to admire the letter and Kenter watched her read, Tolomay leaned against the wall and spoke it aloud from memory. She closed her eyes to bring it clearer to her mind.

Kenter watched her face. He wanted

to shake her. How could he have trusted her so completely? How could she have kept these treasures from him? He suffered worthlessly for moon cycles without them, wasting thought of finding them all throughout his days, totally useless in his new environment, and they were here this whole while? What had she thought in that stubborn mind of hers? That she would keep them from him? She would deprive him? Though he was seething, once her voice struck the air and she read the first words, she had his attention.

"*My dearest child*," she said, "*we are the last community we know of who walk upon this Earth.*

If you stand here you are among the very few whose feet have rested upon this place. If your eyes read these words then know we have fulfilled our burden and have perished, for this sacred chamber is not left without guard.

For a thousand years, we were the historians of this Earth and its protectors. Generation after generation we taught our children all we know. But time changes all things.

We are now the record keepers of

articles that remained undestroyed after the final war. Most are useless now. Electricity and communication have left the world. Solar panels are no longer of use with sun flares so active.

We have managed to retrieve items wondrous to the soul, written word and musical instruments. We stored them for safe haven and have buried them for you to find. We were few among many who cared for these frivolities at the end, but the others have all perished now.

Natural love has left humanity. In man's selfishness he has taken what was not his and replaced it with hatred and murder and greed. Humanity has turned a blind eye to itself through killing machines and war and loathing, but much worse; man has taken away the future of our children by murdering the Earth who offers herself up freely to all who would kill her. To so carelessly murder the one who would cloth and feed and shelter us is an abomination to nature itself, at its very core.

Who would do such harm to a parent who swaddles her children so lovingly in her blanket of love?

You must not put yourself first, before the Earth, no matter how she forgives you, for her forgiveness cannot last an eternity with man's lips suckling the milk from her breast even as it runs dry.

Radiation has crept into her waters and smoke chokes the trees with soot and waste. Her skin and eyes are a wasteland and in her fury she has melted herself from the inside out. Mountains have vanished and rivers have dried. Islands have sunk and buildings have crumbled. She is unrecognizable to us. Earth's children no longer live. We are the last of humanity, we six here before you, and little time remains.

You are the first, so heed our warning. More times of war and fighting will come. We were shown but chose not to stop it, for man's proud control over others has been the Earth's demise. With human hearts hardened, humanity has destroyed all that was once perfect in this world, life.

So if you must kill another, do it only to protect and never for another purpose of your heart.

You must engrain into the souls of each, love of the Earth and acceptance and respect for one another, above all else. Replenish her skin with the spirit of the humanity that we lost so long ago. It is what you are here to do. Relish the moments of joy she offers you.

The destruction mankind pressed upon the Earth will be buried too deep for you to find. Do not effort yourself with trying. We have amassed the last and greatest destruction to touch this world since its beginning. We did so willingly, to afford you no hope to find what should not be found. It is our gift to you. You cannot go back, so begin again and do not follow our lead. The future is the path of your making. Do not cling to the past.

Do not put your faith in others to rule you, not even in my words that steal the emptiness of this page, but rather the depth of your own soul for it is you and you alone who can decide what pathway to make for this world. The actions of your heart are the key.

Find what you can upon the Earth to help aid you in your design, but leave this ground you stand upon untouched.

Do not escape what your heart can reach, my child. One heart in a group of thousands can change the fate of the world. One heart can bring all peoples together. One will. We have seen it."

Tolomay remembered the next words *'She is you'*, but was too afraid to speak them.

"It is you," she said instead. *"The Earth has awaited you. You will know what path to take. The choices are yours, my precious, precious child of spirit and light. You are here."*

Then she fell silent.

All in the pod community were trained of the future from the age of four. They were told of the world's destruction that was soon to come to their pod communities. Using the Pool of Light, the elders regularly searched for holes in time that would allow glimpses of itself, even years before it was put to use for time transport, for Tolomay's swim. All knew what had been seen in the Pool of Light's reflection, the end of a livable world, the death and starvation afterward, and then a time, without humans standing upon the grasses, while the Earth renewed herself.

That was how Tarron Ramey, the Science Division, and the Pod Council selected the time point best to send candidates through to. Those glimpses of the future, as few as there were, answered the most important question ever put to the lips of mankind: how long for the Earth to heal before she could once again support human life?

They had to look to the future. For contrary to its earliest study, everyone knew time cannot be travelled backward. The past mistakes of men could not be fixed. No glimpses of the past had ever been seen. So they had to send candidates one thousand years ahead, to one of the few light points available, to the days in which Tolomay and Kenter and Lethia stood.

Training of the world's demise and studying facts spilled onto paper while children in a pod community felt nothing to Kenter and Lethia like the sensation in their hearts at this place in time. Through the letter contained in the encasement, the facts had been personally written to them by the last of those who survived Earth's destruction.

This was the last letter to touch the hands of living men before the clean world had her turn again, the last letter to breathe the air of the world of men before its end. They were standing on sacred ground, where the last of civilization had stood, in the very same room.   The moment felt a lost place in time and none could speak through it. For the longest while they stood in silence.

"Wow," whispered Kenter, finally snapping the quiet in two.

"Yeah," Lethia agreed.

Then she turned to Tolomay.

"But you spoke it wrong," she said.

Tolomay's heart dropped.

"What?" she asked.

"You did," Lethia defended her words, "Look. It says 'she.'"

It was impossible. How did Lethia know? There was only one Hebren book in all the pods and Tolomay had hidden it at her father's request.

"You read ancient Hebren?" Tolomay asked nonchalantly. It was her attempt to keep Kenter's attention from the subject of "she."

"It was my third study, as a hobbyist," Lethia answered. "Since the age of six, when I was gifted the most ancient of books."

Someone had found Tolomay's book and gifted it to Lethia? Of all the citizens at the pods, how had it found passage to her?

"Oh," said Tolomay.

"What do you mean?" Kenter asked his sister.

Tolomay bit her lip. It was too late. She tried to no avail to keep her heart from racing.

"Look here," Lethia said, tracing her finger across the flat piece of plexiglass to the page beneath. "It says 'one heart in a group of thousands can change the world. One will. The heart of one will bring all peoples together. We have seen it. *She* is you.'"

She stopped to await Tolomay's answer.

"Oh," Tolomay remarked as if ignorant to the fact she'd misspoken. "Hmmm."

"She?" Kenter said. "You're sure it says she?"

His face leaned closer to the page.

"Yes. She," his sister replied and pointed to a line of symbols. "See here? She."

Kenter thought it for a moment. Wait. One. Moment. Had Tolomay just answered a question with one word? *Oh?* Is that what she'd said? *Oh?*... and she'd said it not once, but twice. Her mouth was packed full of words. She never chose just one. Even when upset, she never chose one. Had she just said, "Hmmm?" She never did that.

He watched her out of the corner of his eye while she stared at them both like a four year old child who'd been caught sneaking water. Lethia didn't see. She was re-reading the letter. Tolomay was trying to hide something of it, but Kenter viewed her cowering beneath her blue eyes. She had deliberately misspoken the word *she*, and he knew it, whether his sister did or not. Tolomay knew more.

"Why?" he confronted her.

Lethia looked up.

"Why?" Tolomay feigned innocence.

"Again with one word!" he said, trying to hold his anger at bay. "Why did you not read it right? What more do you hide?"

"What?" she asked indignantly, afraid she would give herself away by saying more.

Kenter was right. She had deliberately misspoken, but that was not why they were here. She was not done with her difficult task at hand.

"Perhaps, it is her," said Lethia.

"What?" asked Tolomay, watching

for his reaction.

She felt his anger as it rose up like a fire.

"What's her?" he asked.

"We have seen it, she is you," said Lethia.

Kenter stared at Tolomay with ferocity, then squinted. She held another secret. He saw it clearly in her eyes.

"What did they see before you came through the Pool of Light, Tolomay?" he accused. "What do you know? Tell me, *now*."

His fury clawed its way out of his stomach as he boiled from her guises, so much so, he did not even shout it. Still, his eyes demanded her answer. What she knew would likely affect them all. She knew something or would not have hidden this place from them, would not have misspoken on purpose. How dare she keep things this important from him! Tolomay borrowed his anger.

"No one told us what was seen," she said firmly. "Only that all mankind would die before the Earth healed itself from their cruelty. That we were being sent as our responsibility, as the new caretakers of Earth a thousand years from our time, to build a community."

Kenter knew all of this, everyone did. He saw truth in her words, but still she did not tell it all. His fury pierced her eyes and because of it, she was put on the defensive, whether she'd misled the reading or not.

"What did they see before *you* came through, Kenter?" She returned the insult, and caught Lethia's concerned eye.

Tolomay was frustrated, but rethought her anger and continued speaking before he could answer. She should avoid further confrontation at present, but she needed strength. Where was her strength?

"This is not why I brought you here," she said calmly.

But Kenter was not calm. She deceived him and still was in some way, and for a reason he did not know. She all but lied to him, to them both. Why?

"Then think it, Tolomay!" he barked. "Why did you bring us all this way? To hear of the desolation of the Earth? To tell us to leave all that is here? All that I need? Speak it!"

She had expected this from him. Perhaps he had *not* been ready to know,

- 286 -

but now she was ready to release her darkest part of it. Her anger would help keep her tears at bay and lend her its strength while she was in its fierce hold.

"Because… before this place I had given up my hope!" she blurted, in an uncontrolled manner. "I had fallen down the chasm and had given up my hope! I was alone in this world and did not care to be in it! Because of that! I missed my father! I was homesick for my community! And no one was here with me!" she screamed, her voice crackling like it never had before. "I did not care to be alone here for any reason! Not one reason!" she screamed hysterically.

Lethia and Kenter knew what she was not saying, and the long silence parked itself between them all. What she was saying was that she had not cared to be alive. She had thought the unthinkable.

Her own words shocked her. After long moments, she reestablished her grip of them; no longer shouting, she continued in the monotone voice she often carried when telling her stories.

"My past grabbed me and held me, no matter how I tried to think of the future. The past and the ease of the community haunted me, and in spite of this beautiful place I could not find my way into it with no light in my heart.

"I felt Tarron abandoned me here. I reasoned he knew what could happen, that I might arrive here alone, and since he chose to send me anyway, that he hadn't even cared. So, in my sorrow and because of it, I left the hill. I did not want the others to find me there, in my cowardess, when they arrived.

"But I could not think to do it, so instead I walked for hours, further and further from the place I had been abandoned by all who knew me most, by Tarron and those I had stood by and watched perish."

Lethia audibly sobbed, wiping the tears away with both hands. Tolomay came back to them from her trance, with a look of empathy in her eye for the female. Then she stepped to the marble wall, rubbed its cold rock with her palm, and looked to the sky.

This time she spoke to their faces.

"When I fell into this place, my knee was badly injured. It would not work right, and pained me to move. I stayed sitting on this floor for a long while, almost a full day. It was hot. I was so thirsty I thought it my throat would close and block out my air, and I did not care."

Kenter glanced at the handprint stained into the wall, and then at the wide scar on Tolomay's knee.

"I thought it I would die here in this chasm, but I was not afraid. It would have been easy to do, just fold myself and sit for a spell until it took me into its breath.

"That night I dreamed of this clean world. I was standing high, almost as if flying as a bird above the grasses and garden, only standing in one place. There were others here. I saw them below, near the garden and houses. The children laughed and played. Males and females alike stood looking up at me. They were here with me on my hill, all of us together in paradise. I held such a feeling of peace in my heart at that sight. I cannot find words to explain. It was as if real.

"I barely slept through the pain of my knee, but I did sleep a bit. When I awoke, I managed only well enough to stand, but felt more assured others would come and perhaps I could wait for them and bear this world in my loneliness.

"Perhaps I could find a use for my

time until they arrived, as I trained to do. I made the decision to return to the hill, but could not find a path up this tower that surrounded me. Even as the sun brushed its light into this chamber, there was no way to leave it. I could barely step, and so stumbled and fell here, upon this tile.

"When the frame rose up, the words touched me. I felt this letter had been waiting for me. It settled my heart. I wanted to be in this world, in my clean world, the one gifted to me, the world where I would be the first to make a path for others to share. I had the strength then to find passage out. It took long, climbing up the wall in cruel pain. I inched my way up it, the whole while my thoughts only on finding a place for my fingers and toes. Then I was out. I was free."

Lethia's eyes followed the faded brown line that ran half-way up the wall, before it disappeared altogether. Tolomay's expression was solemn. Kenter, as usual, grieved pain for her, at least wholly until she mentioned being *the first*. That was the drop that toppled his bucket. He half missed the last of her words now that his mood was directed back toward anger. She allowed them a moment to take it all in, sure he would listen now.

"That is why I brought you two here, Kenter. So you could feel this place and hear the letter. So your thoughts would know for certainty that the future is forward and you cannot carry the pod with you into this world. Lately, you've both clung to it tightly. It is a danger that will drip from your grip, like blood between your fingers throughout your day, if you do not stop."

Lethia wiped her nose with her fingers. She knew why Tolomay brought them. She was right. Lethia, herself, was growing terribly homesick. Tolomay had warned of it numerous times, not to hold the past. Still, Lethia reflected more and more on it with each rise of the sun. It caused her heartache when the memories hovered in her mind, as storm clouds overhead, gathering water.

Even through his anger, Kenter could not deny her words. He talked more and more about things they missed, the community on his mind quite often. It was easier living at the pod. All they needed had been at their disposal. Life there was a breeze, even with the end of the world looming over them.

There was no fault in talking a bit of the pleasantries of the past, he logicked, but to allow the missing of it to affect one's days, was another thing entirely. He understood Tolomay's warning and concern. While he felt no great sorrow himself, they would need to caution themselves, and not allow it to slither into their hearts, especially after hearing her words of this and reading the letter. As angry as he was, the little traitor was correct. Lethia's heart was tender. It might lead her to be depressed.

Still, that was no excuse for her disregard of him and Lethia in keeping secrets. Metal surrounded them here and Tolomay had shown nothing but deceit today. She all but lied earlier and the haunt of it lay deep within him.

On the night he spoke of his task of metallurgy, she'd listened eagerly. She knew its importance to him. Her keeping this place to herself sliced at his spirit. It was a stab he would not tolerate. He pushed his heart ferociously to one side. He'd come to love her after all, and she could hide great things like these?

She did not trust him, so no matter her story of pain today, it would be a long while before he trusted her mouth, unless she explained the other secret that showed in her face. She had deliberately forced a wedge between them. He stared at her cold blue eyes.

Lethia rubbed the wall with her hand and viewed the top of the well. How could anyone climb a wall like this? Was the letter referring to Tolomay?

"What if you *are* 'she'?" Lethia asked.

"Right," Kenter spit his sarcasm at them both, "Tolomay was sent to save the world, from you and me, Leth."

"There are a thousand people in the world by the time *she* gets here, Lethia," said Tolomay.

Though Tolomay denied Lethia's words about her being *she*, what she believed, felt, and knew was the opposite of what she led Lethia to believe. Deep in Tolomay's heart, she knew without a doubt the letter had been written to her personally, and left in this place specifically for her to find. What she didn't know was why, or how. She could not find the strength to speak more on it.

"Perhaps they went mad at the end and none of the warnings are correct," exclaimed Kenter, interrupting her thoughts.

Then he defended the issue of gender.

"Maybe their hand slipped and that's a scribble on the page and not an 'S'. '*He* is you,'" he said arrogantly, as he examined the frame of the letter.

Tolomay felt his anger's burn. He was pompous. Too exhausted to think on it further, she could hold nothing more against her heart just now. She'd shared her worst nightmare with them, her greatest moment of weakness.

Kenter inspected the framework in the stone. There was nothing visible in the form of screws or nails. It was impossible to take this apart without tools. Had she told them the truth of it, he could have saved himself a climb back down. He could have brought metal from the mounds of dirt into the well to pry it open here and now. As it were, he would have to climb up and return with something useful from the top to use as a pry bar.

"It's ancient Hebren, Kenter," said Lethia, addressing his question of *she*.

Her brother was being ridiculous.

"Their letters and words were different than Merican," she explained. "You can't just throw a squiggle on it and turn the word to '*she.*'"

Tolomay looked to the stripped ivy hanging before her. It was time to leave. She grabbed the rope and held it in place.

"Kenter," she said firmly, her eyes racing from his to escape his angry heat. It tore at his insides like a frantic bug in the lamplight.

Kenter would go first, then Lethia, then her. She could smell the sweat of him as he took hold of the twisted vines. It sent rushes down her shoulders. His heat took her breath away. She chose to stifle the feeling. He was so mad.

He dropped his gaze to find its bottom knot for his feet. In front of him, lay the three year old bloody handprint, staining the wall. He wanted to kick it for making him feel pain for her. He thought to ignore this reminder of her story, but he could not, so his anger cooled a bit, but barely.

The higher he climbed, the more his frustration reared its ugly head until he neared the top, and it spat him in the face. Suddenly, he was furious again.

He cared for her as he had never cared before. How did she disregard him so blatantly? Hiding secrets from him was unacceptable! He *would* be taking things he needed from this place today no matter what she said… and this time his thoughts were not of making *her* life easier, but rather his and his sister's.

Who did she think she was anyway, Queen of the Clean World? What did she think… that this was Tolomay's world? Did she think she was *she*? Dragging them all this way to go home empty handed was not what he had in mind.

Kenter's heart always betrayed his logic where Tolomay was concerned, but he would not cross that road again. Not now. He would not fall for her treachery again. He would have offered anything she'd asked for, but her selfish deceit had changed everything.

Lethia's thoughts were a million miles from Kenter's. She couldn't resist petting at the smooth and perfect marble. She was a carpentry architect after all, and had seen none of it here since her arrival, except for Tolomay's poorly constructed hillhouse.

She marveled at the beauty of the stones and the immaculate construction, the mortar drawn so tightly, it lay almost even with the smooth marble squares it held together. She admired it. Then awe took hold of her as her eyes stepped to each handprint, until the markings faded into the marble blocks halfway up the wall. Even with its tilted sides, it truly was impossible to climb. How had Tolomay achieved this?

'She is the one,' Lethia determined. *'It could be no other. One who could climb this wall could hold the world in the palm of her hand,'* she thought.

She wondered if Tolomay realized it.

"Another thing about that letter," Kenter shouted down as he climbed the last of it. "How are these 'more times of war and fighting' going to find us here? There are just the three of us."

Lethia answered without hesitation.

"Perhaps they were referring to you and Tolomay," she shouted back, then looked to Tolomay with a wink, which was returned with a smile.

Even when Tolomay was troubled, Lethia could almost always make her smile. Lethia held the vine tightly as it wobbled, and Kenter climbed out.

"I was thinking more along the matter of Tolomay starting the wars," he answered in a serious tone, throwing Tolomay his angry glare. It was his way of returning the favor of hurt.

She breathed a heavy breath, knowing she would need to explain to him why she misread the letter. Would he loath her further if she did not do it anytime soon? She wasn't up to the task at present. Reading the letter and littering the stone floor with pieces of her pain for all to see had worn her out.

Lethia repositioned her hands and feet on the rope to follow Kenter's path.

"I can do this in my sleep," she said, smiling before her ascent.

Tolomay hoped she would know what to say when the time came to tell him. No one had trained her for such situations, not really, though she thought perhaps Tarron had tried once.

ChapTer Twenty Seven

Kenter was not near Lethia as I swung my foot over the well wall to stand on solid ground. My heart fell to the dirt as soon as I saw him. He stopped walking at his first sight of treasure and was bending down to pick something up.

"NO!" I screamed with such vigor my spirit jostled me. At my panic, Lethia and Kenter froze.

His hands were empty. I breathed relief for it, but when he stood and spun toward me, his face was red, as if it would pop in explosion. Lethia stepped in before he could shout a single word.

"Tell us why," she said, in her usual calm manner, looking to me for answers.

"It is poison," I said.

He wasn't satisfied.

"Why, Tolomay?" he barked. "Because the letter tells you to leave all of this? That does not make it poison!"

He shouted. "You're assuming things based on gibberish written by someone mad with despair!" he bellowed in his loudest voice yet. "I need these items!"

Seething with anger, he turned back to the treasure. This time I ran and grabbed his shoulder.

"No! Kenter! It *is* poison!" I screamed. "It is not gibberish! And the writer *wasn't* mad!"

When he pulled his arm away, fury stared me in the face.

"How do you know, Tolomay? Another secret?" he raged. "You have so many today! How do you know it is poison? In your great and powerful wisdom, you just know? In your photographic memory and perfect learning you memorized even the future of this land?"

He was making no sense.

"Did you memorize all in this place?" he continued. "Did the elders teach you even how to do that?" he bellowed.

Now he insulted my mind, my education, *and* my professors!

"It is toxic!" I screamed back. "You are the one who's gone mad, Kenter, not the writer!"

Lethia stood silent, awaiting my answer. I caught her thought of it.

"Because I have seen its work at hand!" I continued my rant. "There's radiation, or something else in this place... in this dirt... in the water here... all around us!"

I turned my eyes to Kenter's hateful stare. Exhausted and frustrated, I was nothing just now without my anger. I needed it to keep me strong.

"Why do you think our shoes are padded with sticks and leaves... for the pleasant bumpiness of it?" I continued. "How long must you be here before you listen to my words? You do not know of things here! No matter how you think you do, you do not! You are too new!" I screamed.

"And you do not share knowledge!" he yelled back. "If I have gone mad it's *your* cause for it! And to think it, I almost thought I..." he began, then stopped abruptly.

He shook his head with squinted eyes before continuing.

"I do not know that you aren't lying about this, too!" he raged. "I can believe *nothing* you say!"

That was the end! He denounced my

moral code! My heart shattered into a thousand pieces, but it was hidden beneath my anger. There was nothing he had left un-plucked as the heat rose swiftly to my head.

"Show us," Lethia interjected.

She was wise enough to know I would not mention made up tales. My heart sped wildly as they followed my angry stomping to a small marshy area a hundred meters away. He insulted my father's teachings... his raising of me... my moral honor... every ounce of me. My eyes felt as flames as I stared him down and pointed to the marshy pond. Fish could be seen swimming deeper out, fish with four eyes.

"There!" I shouted with gratifaction. "Are you satisfied? Or would you prefer to see through another set of eyes as well? Perhaps your view would be clearer! And in the event you are unaware, *all* fish belong with two eyes, not four. Perhaps you would like to be your own guide now, too, Kenter, since you have been here a whole two moon cycles! How much expertise you must have mastered of this great world, in that incredible length of time!"

"Well, I would not lead as you do!" he screamed. "Walking us about with secrets, withholding from us as if we are infants! I will bring back what I like from here! These metals are not in this water! I will take what I need from the dry Earth."

"No! You will not!"

"Oh, I will," he said, decided.

"Then you will build your own home to sleep in!" I bellowed. "Nothing from this place will leave here, and nothing will enter *my* hillhouse!"

The look of surprise jolted his head back. As he spoke with controlled anger, I felt his warmth slip away from me.

"I am tired of taking your orders," he said in a harsh and serious tone. "Tell them to someone else who still believes your words. I will take what I need, Tolomay. I will do as *I* want from here on."

He would not ignore my lead! He could not! He *had* to obey! He would *not* remove things from this place, against direction of the letter! Vehement anger swelled in my thoughts as I stared down at the marshes. At that moment, I loathed him for hating me. I spoke before he could turn away.

"Are you in need of thirst, Kenter?" I said pointing to the water. "Since you are concerned with only your own and immediate needs, perhaps I should allow you your indulgences!" I said, blind with anger from his hurtful words.

He turned again to the four eyed fishes, and then to me in a way that ripped me to slivers. He puffed out half a breath as if he'd been struck in the stomach by a surprise attacker, and then pain bled down his expression until his normal look had all but vanished. Without a word, he turned and stepped away through the bushes and down the path that led us there. Lethia stood frozen.

What had I just said? What horrid thoughts escaped through my lips? What had I done?

"Tolomay," she said in almost a whisper, her voice lost in disbelief. "...your words."

I heard such great disappointment. It was as if Tarron's teachings came through her sweet tenderness. He would have been so ashamed. What had I said? I had done something terrible and regretted it instantly, but it was too late.

I allowed my angry thoughts to escape from my mouth as if they would melt into the air before Kenter's ears heard them. But they did not. Instead, they sank into his heart and spirit, and I saw them settle there.

I crossed from a place I did not think I could return to. Kenter's heart. I'd meant none of the angry words that just spewed from my throat. Lethia's thoughtful eyes did nothing to clear my regret. If anything, they set the permanence of it into my heart against myself. Tears swelled my vision. Kenter would never forgive me. I should have told them everything, and sooner. Instead, I destroyed our community with my emotions. It was just as Tarron warned me against. Fire burned at my belly and chest. I knew firsthand about destruction, now. I did it myself today, did it to Kenter and me, and even to Lethia. I diminished my leadership and all that we were.

When Lethia set her hand upon my arm, her compassion stung at me. I did not deserve it. I'd ruined everything.

"Perhaps you should explain it to him…" she said, "about the letter."

She knew. Lethia knew I was *she*. I

felt her thoughts of it coming through her look.

"Not today," I answered.

Her eyes bled pity for me. I could not stop them; the tears were coming. I walked briskly away until I found myself running through the vines, and into the wooded area and then for miles after that. I heard Lethia at a distance as she called out to Kenter to follow. She shouted for me to slow, but I could not. I did not want them to see me cry. But no matter how far I ran this day, I could not escape my remorse.

Chapter Twenty Eight

Kenter and Lethia paced their feet. Tolomay had slowed a bit and they afforded her the great space she desired. Lethia knew Kenter was still angry, but so was Tolomay and she deduced that Tolomay had a motive for not wanting Kenter to know about the letter. She mentioned nothing to her brother about it.

"She's gone mad herself, running off," he complained. "Perhaps she's taking us to some other toxic wasteland, to tease us with its treasures as well."

Lethia had never seen her brother like this. It was beyond anger that was ruling his thoughts. Today, he had been cruel. She stopped. It was many paces before he noticed. Then he turned. At seeing her expression, he stepped back.

"What?" he said, more as a statement than a question.

"Do you not think it she has burdens in her heart you know nothing of Kenter? And the ones we do know of, should shame your tongue into submission before you speak another breath."

He knew she spoke truth, but he had given his trust to Tolomay. He'd given his heart to her and she lied to him. She'd crushed him between her fingers as easily as if squashing a bug. He had foolishly invested himself in her, without a thought to realizing how vulnerable he made himself, or to think if she even felt the same in return. She obviously did not. He had thought it all wrong. She could cause him pain, great and immense pain, and would do so deliberately, without a care for it. Now he knew. First, she'd betrayed him with keeping his precious metals from him and with lies and secrets at the well, and her hateful words at the water... he would not forget them. And still she held another secret from him.

"What thoughts slip through your mind sometimes," said Lethia. "How she must have felt bringing us to this place today, brother."

He did not care. He breathed out a

long breath and waited for the approaching lecture. She'd often spoken the word *brother* in this tone when they'd been children. Were it not for his sister, he might not have learned empathy for others as a child. She only said it this way when his sympathy had been pulled from him, as it had been today. Kenter hated it when Lethia spoke in this manner, but though shaming, he always listened on her words. Often, she saw what he missed. She spoke with intense seriousness, and her soft eyes meant to guilt him, just as she always used to when he needed scolding of the very worst kind. But today he was right.

"She lied," he defended himself.

"You don't know that, and if she did, you do not know why," she replied. "Maxy and the Science Team *lied*, Kenter. Those elders *lied*. Wait to find out and to know why before your fury erupts again. She will tell you when she is ready."

Kenter said nothing, but instead viewed his sister with dull eyes as he chewed at his lip in frustration. Never, in his entire existence, had he been this angry. His nostrils flare as if he were a wild beast.

"Your words were wrong too, brother," she continued. "You only made it more volatile. We have had each other to share talks with. Who has she had? Instead, her heart cries to itself. All she has done is task herself to survive, in hopes that more will come."

Kenter kicked a small rock out of his path. Lethia knew nothing of what he felt, of how Tolomay had ripped his heart to shreds without a care to it, how he had thought each day upon his arrival here of finding his metals to help him be the hero of the clean world, to be Tolomay's hero, to use highly prized metals for the tools they all needed. He responded to his sister with a justified clear of his throat. He was right about everything. She was wrong. Lethia shook her head.

"Your hot head steals your spirit at times," she said. "In all honesty, I do not know you today," she finished, and walked on ahead.

Lethia always made sense, but it didn't squash the betrayal he felt, or the words from Tolomay's lips, telling him to find a new home, wishing him to drink toxic water. Nothing worse could ever be said, after all, than to wish ill upon another person, let alone death, especially after the GoldHoarder's mass destruction and their poisoning of others.

One might as well kill another with their own two hands, than to speak of it. He had been mistaken to love her. She obviously felt nothing other than wanting him ill, four eyed, or dead. The tears she wept were merely for her guilt, he reasoned, for her remorse, and for being caught in a lie. It was possible she grieved for her pure lack of humility.

In any event, they clearly weren't for him. It was evident to him now. She felt no loss of spirit between them as he did. She did not want him. He was a fool and her heart was selfish. No matter how much she loved the clean world, she did not love him. His anger protected him just now. He would not forgive her, not for any part of what he had seen or heard today. He would not forgive her for his pain.

~ ~ ~

Tolomay finally stopped, then sat upon the grasses. By the time Lethia arrived, her eyes were dry, but her face was red and swollen and the front of her garb soaking wet. She looked a terrible sight. Every few seconds, her air pulled itself in, in awkward rhythms, as if she could not catch her breath. Kenter held up his chin. She deserved it for cutting him to the core. How could she have done it to him? She kept her distance and did not view them.

"We need to put up the tent," she said, and then sniffed at the wet, to keep it in her nose. "It will be dark soon."

Two blankets were set over a low branch, as a cover to lie beneath, and the third was spread upon the ground as bedding. Kenter cleared the dirt and set logs upon the Earth before starting a fire nearby.

It was an uncomfortable quiet for each of them. Tolomay opened the food pack, then handed Lethia the mixture of herbs to rub on their skin, to ward off the mosquito insects. Though the twins spoke to one another and Lethia tried at conversation with Tolomay, the upset female spoke few words at dinner, and none to Kenter. She had said enough today. She fell asleep after the food. While Kenter and Lethia stayed up talking into the night, Tarron visited

Tolomay's sleep with memories.

~ ~ ~

She was three years old and he was once again shaving her head smooth. The blond pieces fell to the floor.

"Father, why must I lose my hair each time it grows?" she asked. "Do you not like it? Is it ugly to your view?"

Tarron stopped what he was doing and turned to her.

"My angel, your hair is most beautiful. I want to save it for you so you can share your light with others."

"My hair is my light?"

"No," he said touching her cheek. "Your light is the strength of your spirit of heart, my child, but your hair matches its beauty."

Tarron walked to a cabinet and removed a small box. It contained every bit of Tolomay's previously cut hair. She knew where he kept it. He opened it and pulled out a very thin section, whose bottom curled to a ringlet on one side. Cupping his hand beneath hers, he spread her finger's flat.

"This was your first hairs," he said, laying the strands gently onto her palm.

"From when you were an infant."

"But if you like my hair father, why do you keep it in a box? Do you not want my head to share it, like all the others?"

"I keep it so we can weave your dress from it, Tolomay. So you may lead others through the Pool of Light when you are old enough, so you can keep the world at peace for all peoples, my precious, precious child of spirit and light."

Chapter Twenty Nine

As usual, Tolomay was the first to awake in the morning. She viewed the sun rise as it melted away yesterday and watched as Kenter slept soundly.

She never felt so reckless. In keeping the secret to herself so it wouldn't affect their community or more rather herself, as it seemed now, she had done just the opposite. She'd acted in great fear.

Would he always despise her after yesterday's words? If so, it would be her own cause and she deserved it. She had not spoken nor heard such harsh words in her existence as the ones which spilled as a storm from her lips at the swamp.

Why had she said them? Because he'd insulted the core of her intelligence, she decided. Were her mind and her father's teachings more important than another's spirit, as egocentric a spirit as it was? They were alike, her and Kenter, both confident souls as stubborn as gravity.

Perhaps it was not a good thing to have too much gravity all in one place. Nothing would grow. Sitting beside the sleeping male, she was not confident this morn, but she *was* quick to forgive his words of yesterday, because her heart knew he did not mean them. She wondered what his heart would tell him.

When he awoke to her stare, she almost turned away, but instead fixed her eyes upon his. She would draw courage from her heart this morning, before Lethia awoke.

"I'm very sorry for my horrid words, Kenter," she said bravely, smoothing her short hair with a nervous palm.

"Okay," he said, as if nothing mattered, then stood arrogantly and strode into the woods.

Normally, Tolomay would have been angry at his lack of forgiveness, and for his lack of an apology for that matter. After all, his words had been cruel, too. But her remorse was great and so no matter his words, she did not regret her apology.

What he wanted from her was the

logic for her deceit and information. She knew this. She wished she held Tarron's advice at present, but he had not discussed this subject with her and she had not been old enough to ask.

"Good morn," said Lethia, turning to Tolomay as she awoke.

"Good morn."

"Better today?" asked Lethia, rubbing her eyes awake with the backs of her fingers.

The upset female chewed her fingernail and stared at the woods. He would always loathe her after yesterday.

"Tolomay, I heed your words almost always," Lethia said, "because you are wise beyond our knowledge in this place. But I know something of my brother's heart and of these matters. He is easily wounded. You need to tell him first, and then tell us both why," she said softly.

Perhaps Lethia was correct. She was older and more experienced in these matters. Perhaps telling him, even now, was best. In all certainty, her own plan of it had failed terribly.

Kenter stepped from the trees.

"We will speak, right now," Tolomay said, wanting to explain before her fear returned.

His angry heat was still there as she grabbed him by his arm and pulled him into the woods, but he let her lead. Whether she was selfish or not, he wanted answers. It was difficult, so she did not think it first. That way her mind could not change.

"I did not tell you the right words, deliberately," she said, now relieved.

"Yes. I know," he replied with his head held high, "Why?"

"Because I did not want anything to change," she said, terrified.

Kenter did not understand.

"What would change?" he asked, clenching his jaw.

He rolled his eyes at the cold hearted female who stood silent for a moment. Once again, she played her games with him.

"Because I am 'she,'" Tolomay answered.

"What do you mean you are 'she,' Tolomay?" he asked, with a rising tone.

Now, he was even more frustrated. Not only was she selfish, but as arrogant as the sun.

"Because the letter was written to me," she said.

Tolomay *had* gone mad.

"Think it, Tolomay. You may be the first here… the first female here, but look around. There is no one, only us. It would take a hundred years for a thousand people to travel through the Pool of Light, and they would not want a war," he said, wrinkling his eyes to a tight squint. "So, what are you talking about?" he finished.

"I do not know how. But I know this much…" she said, "Tarron sent me the letter."

Even in his fury, he would not bring up the memory of her father with a negative word, or the impossibility of Tarron being alive at the end, but they all knew her father died long ago. Lethia stepped into the trees beside them. She had heard nearly all of it.

"He used my name," Tolomay insisted.

"Ah, yes!" exclaimed Lethia, turning to her brother. "In its origin, Tolomay means spirit and light; its original meaning is exactly that, sound for sound."

"Yes," agreed Tolomay, "and he used to call me 'my precious child of spirit and light' when I was young…in our own tongue. He spoke it all the time."

Kenter refused such nonsense.

"Pssht," he said, snickering. The females were ridiculous. "In all certainty...you cannot believe this, Leth."

"There is more," Tolomay interjected. "Once, he told me that I was to come to the clean world to keep peace between peoples."

"He told you that before you came through the Pool?" asked Lethia.

"When I was three," she answered. "But I remember."

"He spoke to you of a war?" Kenter asked.

Tolomay's eyes found the ground.

"No," she said.

Lethia and Kenter searched each other's thoughts.

"But there is something more," Tolomay continued. "I was by the chamber doors one day, waiting for Tarron to arrive for my training. I was five. A group of elders walked the other side of the lattice wall, the one near the yellow council doors. There were many council members in the room, and a seer who read the reflections.

"Not looking well enough to notice my presence, they spoke freely. I heard them speak of Tarron and me. Because I did not yet know their garish language fluently, I understood little of their words. But Tarron had started my training on that dialect, so I recognized some.

"The ones that stuck in my mind were, 'Tolomay', something to do with 'kissing my father's shoes', 'war', 'sphere', 'pool', and 'wrong choice'. They were arguing about something and it had to do with me and Tarron. I did not understand, and I still do not, but when the men were done, they stepped from the other side to see me sitting in wait on the bench.

"One had a look I have never seen on the face of any other. He loathed me. Deep into his core he hated me; so much so, that for a brief moment my heart feared for my very safety. As they walked away, he turned back again. He had that same look in his eye.

"I did not understand how a person could hate another, especially when they do not know the person's spirit, and I did not know this male. That's why I remember it so well. But Kenter, why

would my name be used in the same
sentence with the word war, unless the
letter was true and they knew something
terrible would come into this place? So
it is me in the letter. I wholly believe it
is."

"And you tell us this now?" he
barked, angry again.

"Kenter… enough," said Lethia
firmly. "Is there nothing else you know
of this, Tolomay?"

"Nothing," she answered.

"All right then," said Lethia. "You
two will need to talk further, in privacy."

Brows up, Lethia glared a warning to
her brother to behave, and then walked
into the sunlight. Kenter viewed
Tolomay.

"Why these secrets? Why did you not
trust me with your knowledge of all those
metals before now?" he demanded.
"And you would keep the fact of a war
from me? Am I an infant?"

He was still mad? Tolomay had
apologized for yesterday, she had told
him her secret now, and still he was mad!
There was no pleasing this stubborn,
bullheaded, spoiled, selfish male!

"What? I told you, now!" she said.

She could not muster the courage to say why again, and so leaned on her frustration.

"Are you in a hurry for war, Kenter? Do you see a thousand people here?" she asked. "Did you really need to know this now?"

"Just answer the question!" he demanded. "What other tricks do you hide?"

She was furious.

"*WHY*?" she screamed as her whole body shook with angst. "That is your question... *'WHY'*? Are you so stupid you do not know?" she shouted and stormed off into the trees.

With a scowl and wide eyes, he breathed out frustration as once again, Lethia came to stand by her brother.

"She *has* gone mad," he said. "She lies and keeps secrets, tells me to move from the house, to drink poison, and now in her selfish heart, she calls me stupid. How did I think her so differently before, Leth? She is wholly selfish."

"Kenter," said his sister, "you are such a great fool. Did you not hear what her reason was when at first she spoke it?"

"What do you mean?" he asked.

"She told you she didn't want anything to change because she was 'she,'" Lethia spoke calmly.

"What do you mean?" he asked. "What would change if she really were 'she'?"

"Think to it for a few moments," she said. "You have only to imagine that she is. I know it will come to you."

At her words, Kenter wrinkled his brows and stood stubbornly, awaiting Tolomay's reasoning to make sense to his mind. His perturbed expression began to melt as wax in the sun when it dawned on him what Lethia meant. His eyes grew wider and his mouth dropped open in astonishment.

Had Tolomay worried about *his* reaction to the news of her elite status as *she*? Had she worried for his wounded pride? Was that her reason for holding back information? She had hidden her secret *because* of him, and not *against* him? His head spun toward his sister.

"She thinks of me?" he said in a whisper, as if to keep it a secret from the air, then his eyes raced to the woods.

Lethia raised her brows in agreement.

"That my heart toward her would be

- 324 -

diminished... because it is not me," he said.

"Finally..." she said patting his shoulder. "The sun shines in his mind."

He stood, deep in the wonder of it. Had his sister reasoned this correctly? Had he been so entirely wrong about Tolomay's secrets?

"Now, perhaps I can find peace between the two of you," said Lethia. "You'd better go find her."

Lethia stepped back to the grasses to leave Kenter with his thoughts, and hopefully both of them to their conversation. Humility filled his heart. He reacted exactly how Tolomay worried he might. He was much too proud; yet, still she loved him. Did she? His heart raced. He would hide his fear from her, and his desperation for her answer; after all, he was the male.

Tolomay's World and The Pool of Light

ChapTer Thirty

Even the smell of the pines did not ease my frustration. Kenter was blind to me and my words. He would never know my thoughts of him and I would never tell him. I had ruined all the greatest things of our community by bringing them to the well.

Regardless of their homesickness, I should not have done it. I should have kept the letter to myself. It *would* take a hundred years to send a thousand people through the Pool of Light. I knew that. He was right. Nothing of it made a day of sense. I sat on the fir needles, my head resting in my hands. War. What war?

Kenter's steps were so loud that every living thing on this planet could hear his feet upon the ground. He was making as much noise as a clumsy beast. Still, I peered backward, out of the corner of my eye, to be sure it was him. I took my hands from my face when I saw him, but did not turn to meet his gaze.

"I will believe you are 'she,'" he said calmly, as he neared. "... if you promise there will not be a war for a hundred years."

What? If this was his attempt at an apology, he was failing immeasurably. Was this his idea of a joke? Now? Here? After yesterday? He wasn't funny. Still, I listened for the rest.

He sat beside me and his warm energy swarmed about me like a cloud of butterflies reflecting their love upon me with fluttered wings. I said nothing.

"What did you not want to change, Tolomay?" he asked.

His question shocked me in an instant, as tingles fell to my every cell. They ran from my face, down my shoulders and onto my arms, legs and feet. I could not answer. My heart raced with passion, and that wave of falling and flying all at the same time took me for a moment. I waited for his next words, but he said nothing. He wanted *my* words. I could not speak them and so they did not come in the long, long silence that hung in the air. But he knew my answer already. He had thought it out. I swallowed. Would he touch my arm again? My hand?

Then Kenter did something unexpected. He stood to leave. As he walked away, words of his heart spilled upon the pine needles. He did not turn back to me, but stopped only briefly. For a moment he said nothing, and then the next, he spoke it all.

"I was afraid it was only me who felt the warmth," he said, and walked back out of the woods.

The air stole my breath and I hadn't even noticed. I gasped it back quietly and chills sped down my spine. As I closed my eyes, joy of relief ran through me. It trickled down my cheeks in warm streams.

His words were apology enough. I was ever grateful. Kenter did not care that I was *she*. It would not infect our community. Nothing would change. And he forgave me for yesterday, as I had forgiven him.

Yesterday's angry words would not tread upon our lives. It was the most either of us would say that day, regarding our hearts, but we knew what it meant. There was a clear understanding between us, no matter how much remained unspoken. We cared for the other; finally, we both knew it.

Sometimes matters of the heart need few words to spill upon them to make things right. Now that he knew the truth of the letter, I could allow his choice of me, if ever he decided to make it.

Chapter Thirty One

The air screamed a horrid pitch, then poured a glowing blue water from itself. Toner's voices hummed through the slit, until three bodies tumbled out and onto the hill. The light point sealed itself shut with a loud and thunderous *clap*.

One male and two females rolled and stood, but the male was screaming while beating his arm. His wrist was on fire.

The female nearest helped, until the angry flame was smothered. His strength left him and he fell to the ground, the skin on his arm covered with singe.

"Bratta!" shouted the female. "Hurry! It's very serious. Oh, Brake."

"Brake!" shouted his sister, kneeling beside him. "Bombs to gravity, you are so burned. Are you all right?" she asked, knowing he wasn't.

She threw her arms around his neck, and began to cry.

"Aaaah!" he screamed. Jerking away from her touch, he shouted to her face. "The med lab! Take me now! Now!"

"It's okay, it's okay," she said as if to convince herself. "You are alive. Claire is with us."

"Kenter! Lethia!" shouted Claire as she scanned their surroundings.

"Where are they?" said Bratta.
Claire viewed Brake's arm with frantic eyes.

"We cannot wait for them," she answered. "He needs wound sap or whistle weed and right now, before the flesh settles. I will search the grasses and trees."

The patch of burnt skin on Brake's arm was peeled up and raw. It oozed blood and mucus from its center. The wound, charred black at its edges, stunk. He shook uncontrollably.

"The med lab!" he cried. "Where is it?"

"I'll find the herbs," Claire said to Bratta. "You two stay. Keep him awake."

Bratta nodded as Claire left down the hill.

"I am dizzy," he murmured, closing

his eyes. "And so tired."

"I'm here, brother."

She could touch his raw skin nowhere in order to comfort him.

"Leth and Kent will come soon. You will see," she said, her voice wrought with fear. "But open your eyes. You must stay awake," she begged.

Neither noticed the figures behind them, until it was too late. Then, they were snatched.

Chapter Thirty Two

Tolomay and the twins detoured to the stream before returning to the hillhouse. It was Lethia's idea to stop and cool off. She wanted to enjoy the end of this travel with the pinks of the sunset against the water.

The grasses welcomed their bare feet before they stepped into the calmly flowing water. Kenter and Tolomay had made amends under the pines, and their knowing carried its joy in their hearts all day. Tolomay seemed visibly nervous at times and Kenter tried hard to conceal his excitement, but Lethia could see it in their minds.

With thought toward hope of one another, their stubbornness had left them both. She was glad for it. She loved them dearly, and hated their arguing more than anything she could think of. But more than that, she wanted her brother to be happy. In all his days, she had not seen him behave as he did around Tolomay, both the fiercely good and the fiercely bad of it.

Kenter's heart raced as he caught Tolomay's look. Her smile forced her dimples inward, and the dimming sunlight brushed her face with a surreal glow. She was most beautiful in this moment, as if she hadn't a care in the world, as if everything here in the clean world reflected its light in her smile. She stood waist high in the stream while the water stroked her skin with its cool comfort.

Closing her eyes, she breathed it in. The day creatures and night creatures exchanged their greetings in the moments of shared space in time, as the sun peeked its last glance over all, causing the ripples to glisten in their desperation to hold onto the light. She loved this world, and was in love with Kenter. Never had there been a more perfect moment. It felt as a dream.

Kenter stared at her. She was breathtaking. Now that he knew she cared, he wanted to claim her as his own. He felt he would tell her soon, once he found his nerve. He wanted to do it before others came.

~ ~ ~

After they entered the house, Tolomay slid the stick from the hole in Carmella's cage. They fed her freshly caught crickets. Lethia removed the water bowl and refilled it, then watched the lizard hop around the skin lined cage in order to catch the jumping black insects. They crunched in her mouth as she swallowed them whole.

"Hey, little one," she said as if speaking to an infant. "Did you miss us?"

Lethia lifted Carmella out of the cage and held her close.

Utterly worn from the day, sleep came only to her as the three lay sprawled upon their bedding. Even exhausted, it took effort for Tolomay and Kenter to settle their thoughts. Watching the other's look, they faced one another, both in awe of their own feelings.

"I meant none of it," said Kenter.

"What?" she asked.

"What I spoke yesterday, I meant none of it. I thought you hid your secrets because you are the first. That you meant to keep my metals from me, to keep me uninformed."

"That is strange logic," said Tolomay.

"I know," he replied, smiling.

"I knew you didn't mean it," she said, "Neither did I. But why do you care so much about being first, Kenter? I did not choose to be first, to be alone, or to be 'she.'"

She pushed the thoughts of sorrow from her mind as she finished.

"It was chosen for me," she said.

"I know," he replied. "Do not be angry with me, do not, but that letter cannot be true, Tolomay. If it were, you would be she, and I would not be surprised, but it cannot be true. I do not understand why it was written at all, the section on war. The rest, yes, but I do not understand the words of a war."

"Neither do I," she answered. "But what I spoke to you yesterday at the swamp," she started and then blinked away the sour memory. "Tarron warned me to mind my thoughts. I lose my strength, at times."

"You lose your control," he teased.

Her beautiful eyes widened. He was

one to speak.

"And so do I," he finished in agreement. "I think it that in the recesses of your mind, you wanted to tell me you are 'she.' That is why you brought us to the well. Am I close?"

Kenter's lips curled to half a grin as Tolomay smiled but did not answer. Would he begin an argument?

"You do believe you are 'she,'" he said, more as an affirmation to himself, than for conversation.

"I believe Tarron wrote me the letter," she replied, firmly.

"Why do you think he never spoke it to you… of this war?"

"Perhaps he thought it would jade my heart. He was very protective," she answered.

Kenter's laugh was so loud, they both turned to see if Lethia had woken. She laid still, the dream world brushing her eyelids with movement. Kenter chuckled as he turned back to Tolomay.

"Your words are so funny," he said.

"Why?"

"Because you can be vicious when it suits you," he said with a great yawn. "And I think it others would need protection *from* you, not else wise."

Tolomay smirked at his teasing.

"Truly though, Tolomay, you have never once struck me as weak," he answered. "Except you run, when you should stay."

His eyes stared at her lips for a moment. Then he breathed in a slow breath before his face took on a more serious tone.

"What do you think?" she asked.

"When others do come, it will not be us alone here," he said rubbing her wrist with his fingertips.

He wanted to kiss her. He wanted all of her, but he was exhausted. He could barely manage the thoughts in his head.

Warmth filled her heart and her breath took her for a moment. She was nervous, but more than that, confused at his words. She watched the sleep pulling at his eyes. Perhaps exhaustion was the cause of his strange words.

"But this is what we're here for, Kenter," she said. "To make a new community."

"But we will not be alone," he complained, then took his fingers away and rolled onto his back.

"Why do you not want others here?"

she asked.

"It's not that," he answered with another yawn.

It pulled one of her own from her mouth as well, and she smiled to herself at his closing eyes.

"Kenter," she said, summoning his view back to hers.

He peeked at her for only a moment.

"Things will be good when others come," she promised. "You will see."

Half asleep, he moaned his indistinct reply.

She stroked the tips of his warm black hair. When something powerful stirred within her, she brought her hands together, nestled them as a pillow beneath her head, and closed her eyes.

Things will be good when others come, he thought to her words.

He needed to grow the strength to ask her for a match while they still had moments to themselves. He wanted an intimate moment for his question. They did not need an audience. He would ask her within days, perhaps tomorrow before the hill. Tomorrow was Tuesday. He thought only of wanting her time, as they both drifted off to sleep.

Tolomay's World and The Pool of Light

Chapter Thirty Three

The next morning the sun crept in with a cloudless sky. Lethia lay on her bedding watching the tops of the trees through the window. She pondered her brother and Tolomay. If they were back at the pod, real dating would be afforded to them, provided one submitted a dating application which was approved by the Senate Council.

It was easier here without those guidelines, but if her brother and Tolomay were ever to match, Tolomay would have no benefit in this clean world of the joy that comes from a real date. Lethia would take it upon herself to arrange it. This was what the female needed, to help fill the pieces of her heart that had broken apart from solitude. She loved Tolomay like a sister and would give her the experience of a date with Kenter, if Tolomay wanted it.

Lethia rose from the bedding and began preparing water for tea. The others slept soundly, and the twin was surprised. The youngest was always up first. Lethia wondered if perhaps the burdens of the letter and hiding her heart from Kenter all these long weeks had kept her from proper sleep. Just then, Kenter awoke. He stared at Tolomay for the longest while as she lay like a sleeping angel. Then he caught his sister's stare.

"She's beautiful," she said.

Kenter, too embarrassed to respond, could not keep his smile from his lips.

"Morning, Leth" he said, and stood to step outside.

Tolomay awoke to find him gone. She rolled over to view Lethia breaking bits of mint into the clay cups.

"Good morn, Lethia."

"Did you sleep well?"

Tolomay nodded as Kenter walked in and then she took her turn outdoors.

"What's for breakfast?" he asked, snooping over Lethia's shoulder.

"You'll see," she said, and handed him a small basket. "Get as many as you can today."

Just as she scooted him out the door, Tolomay returned. He brushed past her on his way out, and they both smiled. Kenter held up the empty egg basket and raised his brows in play.

"Want to come?" he asked.

Before she could answer, Lethia took her hand and pulled her through the doorway.

"I need her help here, Kenter," said the sister.

Hiding his disappointment, he shut the heavy door on his way out. Lethia watched through the window, as he stepped to the distant grasses toward the trees, and then turned to Tolomay.

"Do you want a date with Kenter?" she whispered as if the air was listening.

"What?" asked Tolomay.

Did her ears hear correctly?

"A date, with Kenter," Lethia repeated, "Tolomay, would that make you happy?"

She thought it. The idea had not crossed her mind. Without the council here to approve an actual date, she had not thought it. She'd thought of a match with him, and perhaps someday she would have a child that might look like his father, but a date… how wonderful that would be. Her eyes grew large as excitement held her, only to diminish as she viewed Lethia's long locks. Tolomay's expression changed as she drew her own shoulder length hair through her fingers. Lethia watched the smile leave Tolomay's face. She doubted her appearance.

"He loves your hair," said Lethia. "He spoke it to me, more than once."

Tolomay's eyes remained distant.

"What?" asked Lethia. "What goes through your mind?"

"I haven't a dress," Tolomay answered. "One needs a date dress for a date, do they not?"

"Let's see," said Lethia.

Taking up Tolomay's hand, she started the few steps toward the corner of the room.

"No, Lethia. That dress…" Tolomay protested softly, as they stood at the basket that stored their garbs and skins.

"Wait, now," insisted Lethia. "Shall we see?"

Lethia opened the basket and took the

top skins into a bundle. She tucked them beneath her arm. This woven marvel held every piece of fabric they'd saved, pieces for more blankets, the skins for them to wear, their rags, and the garbs they'd worn into the clean world which were made of their own hair.

Everyone knew only original DNA could travel with a candidate through the Pool of Light. Children's hair was required to be cut and collected beginning at age five, in the hopes the children would someday be selected for the privilege to swim. The hair was reserved to be woven together into fine fabric, like spun silk. It was law.

Tarron began cutting Tolomay's at the age of one. Even when the Pool of Light was shut down, the law remained the same regarding the cutting of children's hair. One's own hair was the most precious thing imaginable. It was a chance for continued life, opportunity to change the future of humanity and to protect the Earth. One's hair was the chance for the greatest privilege ever bestowed upon mankind. It offered one the ability to swim, valued beyond all else, save life itself.

"Lethia, I do not need a date,"

Tolomay tried to convince herself, as Lethia dug further down, moving more gray and red squirrel pelts to one side.

Finally, she reached Tolomay's fine, light golden fabric at the bottom of the basket, or so she thought. She slipped it free from the items surrounding it, pressed on the skins so they would stay their place, and pulled up the blond dress to take a closer look.

Her heart dropped as she began to unfold. It was very small, entirely too short, and extremely tattered, with rips and holes throughout. Large red and green splotches and brown marks driven deep, soiled it beyond recognition of its original state. A large square fell from within the last fold. It was covered in blood stains. This rag had been deliberately ripped from the mother piece. It seemed to have been used as a bandage or tourniquet of sorts.

Lethia hadn't thought it right. The sight shocked her heart. This was a child's garment, a very small, very ruined child's garment. Tolomay was but thirteen when she traveled the clean world and she did not have skins to use right away like the ones she made and gave to Lethia and Kenter. Everything she did when she first arrived, she did in this tiny and ragged dress. It showed.

Tolomay turned away from her memories, her immense joy vanishing in an instant. Between that dress, and the fact she would now not have the gift of a real date, it was too much. Her chest felt heavy, as if all the sadness of the Earth's past sucked at her belly to empty it and then a boulder fell to fill the space. She had not seen that dress in years, and for good reason. She should have burned it, but along with those memories, it held her most precious DNA. She closed her eyes to escape her sinking heart, but it was hopeless.

Lethia gently folded it, set the blond pieces back in the basket and drew out her own dress woven of silky black hair. She palmed Tolomay's cheek softly to regain her attention and handed it to her without another thought.

"Look!" said Lethia. "You *do* have a date dress."

Tolomay's face lit up, if for a fleeting moment. But, she knew Lethia's gesture was too grand.

"Your precious hair," said Tolomay.

"I cannot."

"I will not hear an argue," said Lethia in her sternest voice. "You can and you will. Now, take it! I will have my way in this, Tolomay Ramey. You will use it for one night, and then we can share. I will give you and Kenter a date tonight, so do not worry a thing of it. And your hands must stay clean. I will do today's work in the garden. Just be ready in early eve."

"Lethia…" Tolomay began to protest, but the female interrupted with happy eyes.

"It is *my* day to be stubborn," Lethia said with a smile. "Now, do as I say. Once Kenter comes back, take the dress with you to the stream and try it on to see that it fits enough for your liking."

Tolomay nodded. She had never received a gift from a female, let alone the most precious one could offer, their own travel DNA. She was ever grateful. The fabric felt strong in her hands and she was beside herself with joy. She threw her arms around Lethia.

"Thank you!" she said, finally sounding like a sixteen-year-old. "My heart sings so loudly!"

"Be quick. Hide it so he does not see," Lethia said, as Kenter neared the house carrying a full basket of eggs.

Tolomay's World and The Pool of Light

ChapTer Thirty Four

Kenter noticed something of a change in the air at the hillhouse these past few hours. Both his sister and Tolomay seemed more cheerful than usual. Tolomay's spirit was open today, and he was glad for it. Refreshing to his heart, her normally serious look was replaced by sheer happiness that he had only been allowed glimpses of up 'til this day. His words yesterday had caused it.

He was glad he told her of his feelings for her, though he had not been courageous enough to speak it fully. She knew, though. Both he and she knew what he meant. He made things right again, and now all was much better than before.

But Tolomay's newly opened heart did not explain his sister's odd behavior. Lethia was humming all morning.

"Kenter," she said. "Do you remember the sector twenty dance?"

His sister's question arose out of thin air. He thought it peculiar. He'd gone there on that one dreaded date with the selfish Sandra Lockley. Why did she ask this in front of Tolomay? It was disrespectful.

"Do you remember how to dance?" she continued.

Before he could think it, she stepped up and placed one of his hands into her own and the other at her waist.

Tolomay watched intently to see how it was done as Lethia and Kenter danced in the small space. Lethia hummed to their steps. Kenter was embarrassed dancing with Lethia when it was Tolomay he'd rather be touching. Red painted his face, but eventually he smiled and continued, this time more dedicated in his movements. He would ask Tolomay to dance next, if she would, if she could see how.

"Here, Tolomay. Take your turn of it," said Lethia, before he could speak his thoughts. "I will finish lunch."

Lethia took Tolomay's hand, and replaced hers in Kenter's.

This was the closest physical contact the couple ever had. One hand touched her waist; his large, warm fingers of his other took her hand lightly. He was so incredibly warm. She could not keep her breath as he moved her about the confines of the room. Even when she stepped on his foot, his eyes could not deny their joy. The two danced in silence for a long while, with nothing between them but the air. She was overcome in the grasp of love. Her heart never felt so free. Nothing, not even her affection for this great green world, nor her adoration for Tarron, compared to the warmth his spirit shared with hers. She felt she had known him forever.

Kenter watched her eyes the whole while, even when she turned away from the power between them. Then he stopped dancing, rubbed her shoulder softly, and drew his hand through her hair and back to her shoulder. Her neck was delicate like a swan, her skin smooth and divine. He could hardly hold himself back. He would have kissed her were it not for Lethia being there. He wanted to so badly.

Just steps away in the kitchen, Lethia cleared her throat meekly.

"Lunch is ready when you are," she said.

Kenter wondered what she was up to, setting the couple up to dance together, but he really didn't care. He wanted this kind of closeness with Tolomay from nearly the moment he'd seen her, this delicate heart whose spirit carried the strength of a storm.

The three sat at the table and enjoyed a lunch of eggs and vegetables, sprinkled with wheat beads. They ate until stuffed.

"Whose turn is it to stay at the hillhouse today?" asked Kenter, staring at Tolomay.

It was Tuesday.

"Yours," she replied. "Lethia and I have hill duty."

"No," interjected Lethia as her eyes met Tolomay's.

Tolomay had been correct, but Lethia had something in mind.

"You and Kenter go," said Lethia. "I'll be doing my tasks here today."

"What tasks?" asked Kenter.

"No matter," said Lethia. "Things I haven't gotten to yet."

Lethia and Tolomay shared a glance.

"Okay," said Kenter, not caring what

his sister was talking about.

He was anxious to spend time alone with Tolomay. He would speak it to her then.

Tolomay was nervous as she watched his lips. Of course, she had never been kissed, nor had she kissed, other than her father's cheek. Her heart raced at the thought of it as she watched his mouth take his last bite. She watched Kenter's lips before, wondering what they would taste of and what feel, at the smooth puffs against her own. Would she have the courage to allow it if he set his to hers? She would, she decided, but she wanted nothing of a kiss at the hill today. If it were to happen, she would wait for her date, this eve.

Kenter was in a good mood, too. He helped with the tidying, which was a rarity.

"I'm getting the ropes from the smokehouse. And it needs sorting if we are to use the logs for Lethia's design," he said.

"I'll go...," Tolomay nearly offered to help him, but the discrete shake of Lethia's head, changed her words. "I'll go... over the idea with Lethia," she said instead. "To ensure the two houses will fit together properly."

"Okay," he said suspecting nothing as he walked out the door.

"What are your thoughts?" she whispered to Lethia.

"Whilst you two are at the hill, I will prepare the dinner. Then when you return, do not come to the house straight away. Allow Kenter to come here, but you go to the smokehouse. I will put the basket and dress there for you while you are gone. Then go to the stream and wash up while sunlight can still see your face; use your flower oils, so your aroma will be fresh. And Tolomay, the ancients touched their cheeks with berry juice to freshen their skin and lips. You can do that if you like...but just enough to change the shade slightly. You are pale so do not use too much on your cheeks, or it will look wrong. Use just enough to send his thoughts to them. Barely dab the touch of it, and smooth it well. Is this what you want, Tolomay?" she asked.

"Yes," Tolomay replied. "I want to be beautiful."

Lethia held Tolomay's cheek in her palm.

"You are beautiful. There is nothing

you could say or do that he would find otherwise," she said. "A dress and berry juice is just added enticement. Kenter loves you. Do you not see that?"

Tolomay could not answer, and instead dropped her eyes. The thoughts made her feel weak and she did not like it. She was used to knowing most all things she did and romance was new to her. She had studied none of it, the physical of it, yes, the medical books, yes, the literature on reproduction and birthing and nourishing a child, yes, but she had been an intellectual since birth, since Tarron could first train her. She was emotionally clumsy in these matters of the heart that she had not been trained in. She did not know what she was doing, and felt her lack of confidence growing. Her intelligence and logic were swept away whenever Kenter was near. Would she know how to relax in his company tonight or how to kiss him?

This was the first time Lethia had spoken so directly of Kenter's love for her and the words felt strange to Tolomay's ears. She knew Kenter cared for her, but the word *love* had never been spoken to her other than from Tarron's lips. She wondered if he would tell her of his heart this eve, and not in riddles like his apology in the woods. If he did, could she speak it back?

Lethia saw the thoughts run wild through the sixteen-year-old's mind.

"Stop your thoughts," she said. "You will have fun. That is all you need think to."

Tolomay smiled.

"Do not over think. Just enjoy. There are no tasks or preparation required; nothing you do will not be perfect," said Lethia. "Kenter will be glad just to have the time to spend with you alone, and to see you in a dress. All right?"

Her attempt to set Tolomay's nervousness at bay worked, and it showed itself clearly in her eyes.

"Well, then," continued Lethia. "I will make the berry juice and you can use a skin to set its hue upon your cheeks and lips. Your lips will taste like berries if he kisses you. But take care not to get the juices on your fingers, all right?"

Tolomay nodded. She felt younger than she could remember feeling in a very long time. She was once again the student.

She wondered.

"Lethia," she asked. "Have you been kissed?"

Lethia thought to her secrets, the very ones that violated pod rules and laws alike. None could punish her here for those two infractions.

"Yes," she whispered under her breath. "But please do not tell Kenter. I have kissed twice, but have never been in love." She said touching at Tolomay's hair. "You are lucky for it. I have never seen my brother so happy."

"What was it like?" asked Tolomay.

"It was like a dream."

Lethia filled Tolomay's emotions in a way no female had. She so watched over her heart like a sister and mother and the female was grateful for it.

Kenter returned from his task before the sun told them to head to the hill to wait for new candidates, one's who would likely not arrive.

ChapTer Thirty Five

We lay on the hillside watching the clouds sweep the sky for long moments, before Kenter rose onto his elbow to face me. His eyes spoke to mine until he turned them away to watch his fingers draw circles upon my shoulder. My heart pounded. His touch spread its heat throughout every cell of my body. I'd never felt passion as strongly. The world was painted with love.

"Tolomay," his voice seemed as warm as the sun, my name flowing from his lips as if the breeze through the leaves, as if he had been savoring it and waiting for precisely the right moment to pour its glory upon the air. He brushed my hair from my eyes, ending with his fingertips sweeping gently across my mouth.

"You're lips are soft," he spoke.

My spirit leapt. I was so

overwhelmed tears nearly ran from my eyes. I watched his lips as they neared my face, parted ever so slightly as he took in a breath. Their curl was straightening on their way to my mouth. He would kiss me now. Fear shot through me like a storm, my heart anxious with the untried. I was not ready, not ready to kiss his lips. Though my spirit yearned for his mouth to lay itself upon mine, I was not yet ready. I quickly turned my head away. I would wait until the date, as I had planned.

Rather than a look of hurt, Kenter's eyes filled me up as if I were a precious thing.

"What's wrong?" he asked gently.

I could not speak at first. Even as I took back my breath from the air, my words escaped softly in almost a whisper.

"Wait for me," I replied, sliding from beneath him.

"I will," he answered.

I rose and stepped away from him and into the safety of the trees. My shoulders trembled and my heart pounded. What had Lethia said to me? "Nothing you do will not be perfect," she had said. Should I kiss him now? I felt I would, but so desperately wanted to surprise him this eve, to see the look upon his face when at first he saw me standing in the glorious black fabric of Lethia's dress.

I wanted him to relish the beauty of it, to see me as I had in the stream today. We would both remember our first kiss and I did not want the memory of it diminished by these skins that hung on me like a wild beast, from my shoulders and waist. He would remember the moment. It had to be perfect.

My spirit jumped as the image of our date threw itself into my mind and settled there. The thought overwhelmed me and sent chills down my shoulders and over my arms. I was both nervous and excited and yearned for him. I had to wrestle with my voice to contain it, to stop myself from shouting my joy to the clouds. He would see me this eve as I had seen and admired the beautiful females at the pod, a female in the beauty of a dress. I would wait for this eve to touch his lips, I decided. My heart fluttered at the thought. I had longed for the moment, and it was nearly upon me. I would wait for his kiss. Our date would be miraculous... unforgettable. I loved

Kenter.   Tonight, everything would change.

ChapTer Thirty Six

Kenter watched as I stepped from the woods, his eyes shining their light upon my spirit and his smile into my heart. My lips could not contain themselves as I smiled so widely it stretched at my cheeks. I had never felt such pure love for another.

The wind picked up instantly and the air screamed all at once.

"Tolomay?" he yelled anxiously.

"It's a swim!" I shouted over the piercing noise.

The sound of Tone Men singing burst into the air, followed by glowing blue water.

A body came through at great speed and rolled onto the ground before Kenter. A beautiful female stood up before him in a gorgeous black dress. At first sight of him she wrapped her arms around his neck wholeheartedly, and then pushed her head forward, pressing her lips passionately onto his.

"I knew you'd be waiting for me," she said, and then stood back.

"Sandra," Kenter stood stunned, then spun his head to find my stare.

"You never said goodbye," she remarked slyly, then raised up the hem of her dress up to show him her thighs.

My heart fell deep into the Earth and died there. Blood rushed from my head down and into my toes, leaving a storm in my stomach on its way, my spirit ill with despair. In one split moment dread rushed through me and my joy in this clean world came tumbling to nothingness. It was a dream. This was not real. I was dizzy and could not breathe. I was not here.

Kenter's look screamed of dismay. He knew this female and he knew her well enough their lips had kissed and she had shown him her thighs. My spirit faded into itself and disappeared. There was nothing left of me but the pain of this moment as I stood frozen, staring in disbelief.

Two more bodies burst through the

water before the light point sealed itself closed with a loud and thunderous *clap*. One was a female, the other a male who lay wreathing in pain, as Kenter had when he arrived. I was first at his side and knelt beside him as he screamed his great agony to the world.

"Think to nothing but slowing your breathing," I directed. "Long slow breathing and hush your pain."

"I am dead?" he asked, teeth clenched in anguish.

His breathing was frantic.

"No!" I insisted. "You are burned, but you are alive. Calm yourself and embrace that thought. You are alive."

Then I looked deep into his terrified eyes to force the thought into him, until I saw that he believed.

"Ray! You will be all right," said Kenter, bending down beside us. "I was burned, too. You will heal."

"I am trained in curation and will tend your injuries." I redirected Ray's attention toward me. "But first we must move you. Understand?"

He nodded, and fell from consciousness as I stood.

"Pick him up!" I shouted.

None, but Kenter, moved.

The females stared at me as if all that had been wrong in the world lived within my skin, as if I, the blond GoldHoarder, worshipped death itself. They feared me.

"Come on!" shouted Kenter as he took up the male's shoulders.

At that, the female nearest Ray seemed to wake from her shock. She lifted his feet. The one who'd kissed Kenter stood idly by, watching us lift the male's heavy body. Hatred poured into me at the sight of her motionless beauty. I readjusted my weight and pushed Kenter away with my shoulder. He released his grip and stared at me as if I was on fire.

"I am strongest," he insisted.

He was wrong! My hatred at that moment was stronger than he could ever be!

"The aloe!" I barked forcefully.

Disbelief held his face. I was closed off from him now and he knew it.

"Tolomay," he began to argue.

We didn't have time for his guilty eyes.

"Go!" I screamed as if I'd lost all good sense.

"He will live, Reasha," Kenter said to

the one at Ray's feet. He glanced at me before turning to leave for the aloe sands.

The female and I continued to carry Ray toward the hillhouse. I watched with each step I took as the useless one followed Kenter like a tail.

"She's a GoldHoarder!" she accused loudly, for all to hear.

"No, Sandra," answered Kenter.

"What's wrong with her look and where did she come from?"

"Go help the others," he directed, but she ignored him.

"Why do you let her scream at you, and what happened to your face?" Sandra finished.

"Be of use!" he answered, and walked away.

Reasha and I stepped awkwardly down the steep part of the hill. As Sandra approached us, Kenter turned to view me, but I could not bear his traitorous eyes, so mine fled to the ground.

This female named Sandra was foolish. Her thought to help was to lift the male at the small of his back. All that did was to raise his torso and buttocks several centimeters. She was not strong enough to hold position, and instead shifted his weight to the left. It nearly caused me to lose my grip.

"His other shoulder!" I commanded.

She let loose of his back and stared at Kenter in the distance, as if contemplating choices.

"Please!" screamed Reasha.

Sandra moved to stand at Ray's shoulder. I gave her space beside me as we carried him down the long walk and to the front of the hillhouse. She smelled of the sweetest perfume and I loathed her for it.

"Lethia!" I shouted, out of breath as we approached.

Her eyes flew to the injured male as she opened the door.

"Raymond!"

"Vinegar and wound sap!" I urged her to the kitchen.

She retrieved a bowl of vinegar, brought the water, and began to grind the herb as we settled Raymond upon a blanket.

"Kenter was burned too, Reasha," Lethia spoke reassurance to the sister.

Lethia turned to me.

"Where is he?" she asked.

I hid my eyes from her as I worked.

"Getting aloe," I answered.

"I'm glad to see you, Lethia," said Sandra in a tone of delight, as if this were a festive gathering.

Lethia ignored her while I poured in drops of water and she stirred it to paste.

"It's most serious, here. All throughout his chest and legs too, see?" I said, pointing out the darkest red areas of his skin.

He was burned as badly as Kenter was, perhaps worse. At the least of it, he had larger patches of them. The female named Reasha cried in desperation as her brother passed in and out of consciousness. Lethia brought an arm of comfort around the female.

"He will likely be all right once the paste is applied and Kenter brings the aloe," I said.

"Are you certain?" she asked, staring at my look.

I pushed the rabbit skin deep into the vinegar, forcing it down with my fingertips. It drank up the liquid until it was soaked. He did not wake when I rubbed the smelly mixture upon his face, but his breathing was evenly paced. I leaned forward and set my cheek against his chest. His heart beat sounded steadily.

"We will help as we can, but I believe he will heal from these wounds…" I remarked "if I can keep his shock at bay. I will bandage him and give him aspir for pain so he can sleep. He will need several days with nothing but rest. We must each take turn watching over him, only do not touch his skin or the wrappings once they are placed."

"Reasha," said Lethia. "Tolomay is a wondrous healer. I believe she could have taught Mize."

Reasha's suspicious eyes held mine before settling on a look of gratefulness. Sandra just stared at my golden hair as I spread the wound sap over the burns.

Kenter returned with a hand full of aloe. He had hurriedly picked them and their gel oozed down the bottom of his palm, onto his wrist. I snatched them without so much as a look to his face. I was focused on my task. Nothing else mattered.

But then he knelt beside me, as if he belonged there, and a desperate feeling crowded my throat. I could not allow it. Longing to forget what I had seen, I forced my tears inward. Not here. Not now. I swallowed hard until emotion left me.

"Stand away," I told him harshly. "I need room."

I scraped the gel from one leaf, mashed it in the bowl, and then scraped another.

As Kenter stood, Lethia brought fresh skins for bandages. The paste was nearly set as I began smoothing the aloe onto the most severely blistered patches of tissue.

Sandra stepped near Kenter as if no others were here, so close it was as if she would whisper in his ear, and my heart fell to pieces in my hands. My trembling fingers would not calm themselves as I tried to place the bandages. My adrenalin had slowed and the horror of their kiss crept into my thoughts.

It stole what little strength I retained over my heart. I glanced up at her. Pain clawed at the wall of my chest. Was this what he meant when he said we would need time alone before others came? Had he been in love with this female before he swam? Had he promised to wait for her?

Perhaps he had thought of her his whole while here and his feelings for me were a simple replacement until she arrived. After all, I had been the only available match for him until now.

I looked at her thick flowing hair. It was even longer than Lethia's. Her clean shaven legs were as tall as a tree. Her bosom was amply proportioned. I had none of these to offer him. It was no wonder he had waited for her. She was the most beautiful creature I had ever seen. Never before had I felt so small. I was diminished to nothing. My hands shook as I applied the bandage, and the male awoke to his shout.

"Ahhh!" he screamed.

I tried to control my shaking, but the bandage pressed harder this time.

"Aaaaaah!" he screamed louder.

I hurt him in my clumsiness. Lethia looked to me and then at Kenter and Sandra, and knelt down beside me.

"I have this, Tolomay," she said, offering to finish the task.

I could not leave the patient. As healer, I could not let him die like my team had. Lethia removed the bandage from my hand and held my trembling fingers in both of hers until she drew my gaze.

"I know wrapping as well as you," she said in pity, as if she read my heart.

I rose, useless to them all, now, useless to my community. Except for upon my arrival here, I was less than I had ever been. I watched Sandra touch Kenter's arm and his eyes fall to her fingertips and felt myself being pulled from their presence. It was as if an invisible spirit led me out the door and into the twilight, and my feet could not keep up with its fierce pace. I could not be there with the one who ripped my heart from my chest and reveled in its replacement. When Kenter shouted my name, I ran from his voice and down to the smokehouse.

I could not see him, not now. My back settled against a surviving piece of wall near the logs he had stacked just this morn. Not a tear escaped. I refused them their glory. The only thing present of me in this place was the breathing of the air in my lungs and the death of my heart.

TOLOMAY'S WORLD
and
The Mountain of Tegi

M.E. Lorde

Chapter One

"Tolomay!" he shouted as Sandra grabbed his arm.

"Kenter?" she sounded decimated, her meaning clear. Would he leave when she'd only just arrived?

Snatching his limb from her grip, he threw raging eyes.

"What did you do?" he screamed with force. "Did I invite your touch? Any of it? You don't know of it! You imbecile!"

"Kenter!" she said, stepping back, her wounded look replaced with arrogance.

The injured male moaned his pain to Lethia as she continued to wrap the wounds, but her eyes watched Kenter and Sandra; her ears listening intently to every word. She never liked this female at the pod community who was selfish, manipulative, arrogant, and had been coddled by her scheming father her whole existence. They even looked alike. It spoke rather clearly that cheating had occurred in the DNA tubes, as if Sandra's parent knew ahead of time he'd be approved for adoption and wanted one of his 'own', something which was highly illegal. Sandra began chasing after Kenter since about the age of ten. She even tried to falsify a friendship with Lethia, her only thoughts to gain an advantage to get close to her brother. Lethia was far too wise for that. She saw it for its truth, and never allowed the company of one so shallow as this one.

Lethia warned him against accepting her dating application, but Kenter had not listened because of her appearance. She was the prettiest at the pod. On their first date, even he saw enough of her real person to make him more than leery of a repeat event, no matter her looks. Sandra had not let him in peace since. Now here she was, ruining his chances with someone as true and pure as Tolomay.

Lethia glanced to the patient, then back to her brother. She did not know what happened between Sandra and Tolomay upon the hill, but whatever it was, it had not been good. Tolomay's spirit had all but left her. Even without details, Lethia wanted to slap Sandra's face. This was something she never before felt the urge to do to another. Instead, along with Reasha, she sat listening as her fingers continued their tasking on the moaning Raymond's burns.

Ignoring his words, Sandra reached toward him.

"You bombshackled miser from sulfar pits! Are you dense? Do not touch me again!" he said through gritted teeth.

Her eyes grew large at his swearing. When he ripped himself away and turned to the door, Lethia did not reprimand him for his tongue. Instead, she stopped wrapping.

"Look in the smokehouse," she said. "She will be there."

"Why are you angry with me?" Sandra pleaded. "...and over the crazed look of a GoldHoarder?"

As he disappeared into the night, the female's intent was to follow.

"SANDRA!"

The newcomers were startled; even Raymond jumped in his skin. It stopped

Sandra, who turned to the source. Lethia dropped the bandage into the bowl and aimed her finger to a point.

"YOU..." she glared at the trouble maker. "will stop your feet and sit down NOW!" And the voice that never shouted, bellowed and was heard. "You know nothing of things here!"

Sandra shuffled the few steps to the kitchen and sat on a stump.

"What a horrid, angry world," she muttered, under her breath.

~~~

Tolomay slowed her breathing as she watched the berry juice drizzle from the tipped bowl. Its remnants lay wet upon the smokehouse ground, refusing to settle into the packed down dirt. The basket Lethia had left sat upon the wood pile, the dress waiting for her to slip on. She rubbed its fabric against her cheek.

Her heart ached as if skewered; her dreams lay as broken branches after a storm. This emotion was far too great to bear.

That female kissed his lips. Sandra appeared in all her perfectness and they kissed right in front of her. The moment replayed itself over and over in her mind. She could not stop her thought to it. Never had she felt pain such as this, not even in her greatest despair here. She could not think it to return to her hillhouse, not with the two of them standing there, and the gorgeous Sandra touching at his skin.

She fled into the sunset and down to the bank of the distant stream, where just hours before she was feeling bliss and splendor in the wake of the day, her thoughts toward their date.

Tolomay's World and The Pool of Light

M.E. Lorde

~About The Author~

An avid reader since birth, M.E. Lorde's passion has always been the written word.

The Pool of Light is the first novel of the **Tolomay's World** series by M.E. Lorde

She hopes you will thoroughly enjoy your Travels in **Tolomay's World.**

Special Thanks to:

Kayla F. and Aristea F.

(For your listening and
encouragement))

My mother
(For her wonderful support)

Camtasia Studios-SmithTech

(For Video Software)

M.E. Lorde

TOLOMAY'S WORLD

~ Series Books~

(First four of a Seven Book collection)

The Pool of Light

The Mountain of Tegi

The Splitting of the Trunk

The Wall

Tolomay's World and The Pool of Light

M.E. Lorde

Made in the USA
Charleston, SC
09 February 2014